MORE THAN ONE NIGHT

a Heroes of the Night novel

Nicole Leiren

D1444053

For my husband and daughter, who understood and supported my need to spend countless hours tucked away in an imaginary world and who didn't think I was totally crazy because of it! I love you both so much!

Acknowledgements

There are so many people, friends and family alike, who have played a part in making this story become a reality, I couldn't begin to name them all, but I am grateful for each one of their influences in my life.

I would like to extend a heartfelt thank you to:

My parents, who taught me the love of reading and the power of the written word. Your unfailing belief in me from the very beginning has taught me that believing in myself, working hard and never giving up makes even the most distant dreams seem possible.

My little sister who, whether she knew it or not, encouraged my creativity by insisting we play "make believe" ALL the time.

The Windy Cityzens from my RWA group for the mentoring and unfailing support you've given me since my very first meeting.

My critique partner, Vanessa Knight, for the countless hours you devoted to helping me and my manuscript make it to this point.

Dave—thank you for planting the seed for this story in my brain with your story telling. I hope you find your "Melodie" someday!

Dawn Dowdle and Gemma Halliday—thank you for your patience and understanding throughout this whole process. You've made my first time an amazing experience!

Finally, to the men and women who sacrifice time with their families to keep us safe and protect our freedom each and every day—you are the true heroes. Thank you!

CHAPTER ONE

———

Naperville, IL—January 6

Melodie Alexander stood in the dressing room praying she'd thought of every detail. She needed—no, wanted—everything to be perfect. Tom deserved nothing less than her very best. Her simple dress, accented in delicate lace, fit her petite frame like a glove. Her best friend, Lydia, had taken extra care to style her wavy dark brown hair in an updo she claimed softened the angular lines of her jaw. Small combs worked to hold wayward strands in place. The roses, Tom's favorite, were held tightly in her grasp.

Drawing in a deep breath, she fought to calm her jangled nerves. This was not the way things were supposed to turn out. Not at all. Tom was her best friend. They'd made a pact. If neither was married by age thirty, they'd tie the knot. Only six months remained until the significant birthday. An errant tear threatened to slip from the corner of her eye, and she hastily dabbed the offending moisture.

Before thoughts of Tom distracted her any further, she glimpsed in the mirror for one final check of her makeup. The right hint of color tinted her otherwise pale and lightly freckled skin.

The door quietly opened, revealing her father. "Are you ready, baby?"

Ready? The nerves in her stomach began their familiar dance. Nerves, along with a purveying sense of dread, settled deep in her heart. Could she really do this?

Soft strains of classical music filtered into the vestibule as she approached the room where everyone awaited her arrival.

As the doors opened, every eye riveted to her trembling frame. Her steps faltered slightly, the rapid beating of her heart making it difficult to remain calm. She clutched her father's arm, drawing from his strength as she had in her youth. Her breath caught as the emotions of those gathered overwhelmed her. The intensity of their focus prickled her skin, creating a fine sheen of perspiration. Her limbs, stiff with nerves, made each step laborious. For very few would she endure being the center of attention, but for Tom...anything.

The long walk over, she arrived at the front of the church. The comfort of her father's embrace enveloped her for a moment longer before releasing her to take his place by her mother. She wanted desperately to place a kiss on her beloved Tom's cheek. Instead, the minister cleared his throat, indicating they could no longer delay.

Turning toward the sea of faces, the fierce grip on her composure loosened despite the desperate fight to not lose the battle. Not here. Not now. She blew out a slow breath, certain her emotions mirrored theirs. Keen. Intense. Overwhelming. As if every ounce of love she'd ever experienced—ever could experience, ever would experience—was trapped between the four walls surrounding her, closing in on this exact moment in time. Today she couldn't hide behind the shelter of the fictional world she retreated to when life became too much. Oh, how she wished she could. It would be so much easier to believe this was just another book she was reading and not her life.

Exhaling deeply, she spoke to the waiting mass. "Thank you for coming today to remember Tom and the ultimate sacrifice he made for his country."

CHAPTER TWO

Chicago, IL
Saturday—September 6

"We will now begin boarding Flight 203 with service to Dallas, Texas. All executive, platinum, gold, and uniformed military personnel are welcome to board at this time. Please check your boarding pass and step forward only when your group number is called."

There was a time when Daniel Bresland would've boarded with the men and women serving their country. He'd been so proud wearing the uniform responsible for transforming him from a boy into a man—a man willing to put his life on the line to fight for freedom and the American way.

Even though his frequent trips abroad during his stint as a civilian contractor earned him status to board with the initial group, he wouldn't dishonor the men and women still fighting a war many believed no longer necessary by considering himself worthy of joining them as they headed off to their next duty assignment. Saddam—dead. Bin Laden—dead. No nuclear devices found. Maybe Joe Public was right, and there wasn't a legitimate reason for being there. To a soldier, though, logic didn't matter. Soldiers followed orders. The soldiers who'd followed his orders had paid a steep price for a system trusting those in a rank above to make the best decisions.

He swallowed hard and pushed back the anguish threatening to rise to the surface of his carefully constructed façade. *Not my fault.* At least that's what the review board had determined, along with the army shrink. They had all forgiven him and said he wasn't to blame.

Too bad he couldn't forgive himself.

His phone buzzed, and he glanced at the screen. If it were anyone else, he would've ignored the call. "Hey, Princess."

"Hi, Daddy. I miss you already!" The sweet voice of his eight-year-old daughter, Annie, made him smile. Even though he'd just spent a week in Mississippi with her, his heart constricted thinking how much time would pass before he'd see her again.

"I miss you too. Are you being good for Mommy?" The question really should have been 'Is Mommy being good for you?' but he'd promised himself never to speak ill of his ex-wife, even if her parenting skills ranked well below adequate. Oh, she loved Annie. He didn't doubt that for a second. Unfortunately, her love of the bottle often pushed their daughter to a sad second place in her life. Now that he was a civilian again, joint custody was on the top of his list of goals for the rest of the year.

"I'm always a good girl."

He could practically see her smile and bright blue eyes. "Yes, you are. I'm getting ready to board the plane, but I'll check in with you later. I love you."

"I know, and I love you too."

"Now seating all passengers, all rows. Please board at this time for an on-time departure."

Daniel handed his boarding pass to the gate agent. As he walked down the jet bridge, a vehicle backfiring from outside triggered the memory he fought hard to keep buried. Cold sweat beaded on his forehead. *An explosion, the ringing in his ears, the screams*—memories refusing to be buried with time. Each horrible detail from that day always travelled with him. Today, the trip was made even longer by a connection in Chicago rather than flying direct to Dallas. He needed a drink. Not the best way to drown his sorrows as it only masked his guilt. It would have to do until he could meet up with Alana, a fiery redhead he could lose himself in. An image of her, dressed in nothing but red lingerie and holding a bottle of Jägermeister, flashed in his mind. She would make him forget and ease the pain. He sighed. It was never long enough.

* * *

Melodie boarded with group three as instructed and made her way to row twelve. She carefully looked at the diagrams to make sure she sat in the proper row and seat—12B to be exact. Her research on the seating for an MD-80 had yielded confusing results. The seats, two on one side and three on the other, were labeled *A*, *B*, *D*, *E*, and *F*. The lack of a *C* seat would make for some fun future research. This was it. She was finally doing what Tom had always encouraged her to do: Go on an adventure. Her mother had fussed, but she always fussed. Going on a trip alone was well outside her comfort zone—well outside the pages of her favorite books. Tom had been gone for over six months. It was time.

She buckled in and properly stowed her purse under the seat in front of her when a Southern-tinged voice interrupted her internal checklist.

"Excuse me, ma'am. I'm in seat *A*."

She drank in the tall glass of sweet tea standing beside her. His thighs were at eye level, providing a close-up view of muscled legs sporting faded and ripped jeans. She focused on the area where those jeans fastened. *Down, girl! What's wrong with you?* The fabric of his T-shirt clung to his abs and chest as though his body had been poured into the shirt like a mold—an incredibly ripped mold. This man belonged on the cover of a sports magazine. She moved her eyes upward.

His cocky expression sent an easy-to-read message. I'm sexy, and you know it.

Heat suffused her face as she fumbled with the buckle on her seat belt. She stood quickly, not accounting for the close quarters inherent in airplanes. A fraction of a second later, she was up close and personal with the subject of her study due to a less-than-graceful fall. "Oh…" Her breath hitched when the solid mass of chiseled flesh countered her softness before balance could be restored.

"I'm sorry." Her apology sounded lame, maybe because the tingling in her body from their collision made her a lot less sorry than she should've been. She avoided his intense blue eyes until she could finally get her uncooperative feet under her enough to step out of the way, allowing him to pass.

What the hell? He's eye candy. Tom was boyishly cute. This man...well, "boy" wouldn't be a word ever used to describe him.

"No apology necessary, ma'am."

His Southern accent caused her body to swoon in the seat. City boys, sadly, didn't talk that way. She refastened the seat belt and tried to regain composure, not an easy task. Her skin tingled everywhere their bodies touched, making her feel alive, more alive than she'd felt in months. Deep breath in, deep breath out. Instinct surfaced and issued a deafening shout in her ear. *Avoid this man.*

She bristled from the internal warning. Where exactly had instinct gotten her thus far? Alone and hiding from life. Time to act on her promise for change. Gathering her confidence, she turned and extended her hand in his direction. "I'm Melodie. Melodie Alexander. And you are?"

The earlier heat from her face expanded to cover most of her body as his gaze swept across her with unabashed curiosity, increasing the prickled skin to full-fledged goose bumps and the thudding in her heart to triple time.

"I am in need of a drink." The charming tone of his voice had changed to a pained admission.

Crash and burn. All newfound courage and bravado vanished in a fraction of the time taken to build it. The heroines in the books she read never got shut down by the handsome hero or, if they did, a quick-tongued and eloquent comeback would leave the hero overwhelmed with his need for her. A quick glance out of the corner of her eye revealed her proverbial hero staring out the window. No overwhelming need, not even a second glance from Mr. Magazine Cover.

Life is different outside the pages of a book.

Her old friend, insecurity, resumed its foothold on her heart. Strike one for the new, adventurous woman.

Time to return to the familiar—the comfortable. Before she opened the pages of a book, a companion she never went anywhere without, she managed one more look in his direction. "You're not the only one."

CHAPTER THREE

The sadness in her voice sliced through the first layer of bitterness around his heart designed to prevent any doe-eyed, innocent-feigning women from getting too close. He'd been rude to a polite woman introducing herself. What the hell was wrong with him? *The memory... the pain.*

She'd checked him out though. Couldn't blame the woman for her interest. Oh and she liked what she saw. No doubts there. He could spot interest a mile and a half away. His spine straightened, and his chest puffed out a little. He liked the way her eyes had darkened as they swept over his body. He loved imagining her hands following the same path as her eyes...losing himself in her could prove distracting.

Another of his body parts started the switch from "at-ease" to "attention" as the blood in his body surged southward. *Proceed with caution.*

A fresh layer of guilt smothered the best parts of his fantasy and calmed the appropriate body parts. He heard his momma fussing all the way from Mississippi. *Don't be a jerk. Make it right.* He watched her covertly, while the flight attendants completed their final safety briefing and checks. Avoiding the normal areas his eyes targeted when checking a woman out, he focused on the apparent tension oozing from every pore in her body: clenched jaw, hands gripping the armrest, and white fingers from lack of blood flow, leaving them as pale as her creamy cheeks. Cheeks he wanted to touch. And there went his rogue body part making a comeback effort.

The comforting power of the engine lifted the metal beast into the air, climbing and soaring higher than the birds. His heart rate increased, providing soothing endorphins. Almost as good as a ride on his Ducati—almost. Speed. Power. No time to think. Pure instinct. *Escape from the guilt and pain.*

The woman's slow exhale next to him brought him back to the task at hand. He pried her fingers off the armrest and shook her slender hand. "I'm sorry for my rudeness earlier. I'm Daniel. Daniel Bresland. And you," he pointed to the other hand still holding the armrest tightly and smiled, "must be afraid of flying."

Her pink lips, turned up just enough to classify as a response, reached into his heart, turned up the heat a few degrees, and melted some of the ice settled deep in his chest.

The smartest thing he could do would be to order the drink he'd been thirsty for since he left Mississippi, close his eyes and fantasize about Alana's fiery red personality consuming him and his pain until exhaustion set in, and the nightmares would leave him alone long enough to rest. Yeah, that would be the smart thing to do.

Too bad he'd never been smart—especially when it came to women.

"I've found a little liquid courage helps with fear. Can I buy you a drink when the cart comes around?"

Slim fingers, he tried hard not to imagine caressing his body, released their death grip and flexed a few times to restore circulation. "Sounds like the best offer I've had in months. Thank you."

Daniel nodded, stifling the urge to comment on her lack of offers. "Travelling for business or pleasure?"

"Pleasure, I suppose."

Way too easy. "Not sure if he's going to be good or not?"

Melodie snapped her gaze to his. "What do you mean?"

Damn. What was it about her eyes? She'd suck at poker as her emerald irises reflected a "tell" for every emotion swimming around inside her gorgeous head. "Relax, just teasing. You always this uptight?"

"I…no…I'm just not good at reading people. Sorry."

"Well, I'm not complicated to read. I'm interested in having a good time and enjoying myself while in the company of a beautiful woman." The knife of guilt twisted in his gut again.

He wanted to be more, but the pain of the past year kept him from moving forward.

She lowered her head and shook it slowly. "Nice try."

Of all the people he could have sat next to on the plane, he had to pick Miss-Beautifully-Complicated-and-Shy. Thankfully, he was saved from an immediate response by the flight attendant moving the drink cart next to their row.

"May I get y'all something to drink?

"A Vodka and tonic for me and whatever the lady would like."

His attention diverted away from the blonde-haired flight attendant when Miss Complicated lifted her head. Dark brown waves of hair with a hint of red underneath begged for him to run his fingers through the softness. He made a fist and squeezed tightly to stop his hand from following through.

"Vodka and cranberry, please."

"Sure thing."

Less than a minute later, the beverages were resting on the tray tables. "Y'all enjoy yourselves, and I'll be back to check on you in a bit."

Daniel nodded and poured a generous portion of the vodka into the plastic glass before adding a bit of the tonic water and gesturing for a toast. "So, Melodie...Melodie Alexander, shall we toast to flying the friendly skies?"

They touched the two plastic glasses together in a symbolic clink to complete the toast. Daniel tried to enjoy his beverage, but Melodie's full pink lips, now wet with the alcohol-laced juice, drove his over-active libido into second gear. Though seated, he guessed her height to be a little over five-and-a-half feet as she stood almost six inches shorter when they were fumbling around to get in the proper seats earlier. He dared not even try to guess her age. Women got very pissy when you messed that one up. The last thing he needed was another woman irritated with him—especially one he couldn't escape from until the wheels touched down in Dallas. Her breasts wouldn't win any wet T-shirt contests, but the swell under the soft purple blouse captured his attention and made his mouth water.

His keen vision paid off as he caught a glimpse of her freckles hidden mostly from view. *Down, boy.* This would lead him to trouble as sure as molasses melts and sticks to the bottom of your shoes. He forced his gaze away and back to his drink. "Any special plans for your time in Dallas?"

Crimson colored her flesh, extending his focus on her. Why couldn't he just leave her alone? Walking away had been his mantra of late. The moment her face turned toward him, he understood—a kindred, troubled spirit. Though he had no clue what pain she was trying to bury, he recognized the look in her eyes easily. He saw the same expression every time he looked in the mirror.

"A little history and, hopefully, some fun. I've spent entirely too much time in the present lately, and," her gaze bore into his, "it's been entirely too long since I had any fun."

"You're a history buff?" His voice jumped almost an octave as his pulse quickened. Maybe a troubled past wasn't the only common thread between them.

"I've read so much about our history, and I'm fascinated. Mother talked a lot about Kennedy's assassination when I was younger. She was eight when he was shot, and it created a memorable impression on her. I want to visit the JFK Memorial while I'm in town."

His gaze held hers and wouldn't let go. He'd served his country for two tours in Afghanistan and another stint as a private contractor because of his love of America and everything she stood for. "History was my favorite subject in school. American history." His smile widened. A woman with a shared interest—an interest that didn't revolve around sex. Maybe there was hope for him yet.

This time the corners of her mouth turned up a little more. Progress. God help him if she ever gave him a full-on smile with teeth. He might have to introduce her to the mile-high club. This woman could spell trouble for him in capital letters. He only wished he knew how she'd found a way through his protective barriers.

"Always nice to meet a fellow American history buff."

"Let's go together." The words slid out smoothly, not even slowing down to consider how he'd save face if she said no. *Or, God help me, if she says yes.*

CHAPTER FOUR

———

His invitation sent bells of alarm tolling through every pulse point in her body. Each chord reminded her of why taking him up on the offer wasn't a good idea. *Ding—you just buried Tom a little over six months ago. Dong—you just met him. Ding—he's not your type. Dong—you aren't spontaneous.* The hand closest to the aisle restored its death grip on the armrest, tightly forcing her mind to still the chimes of indecision and doubt.

No more hiding in the shadows. "I'd love to."

His smile reached all the way to his beautiful eyes. "Good." He paused for a few moments. "You like to dance?"

The heat on her face climbed another degree or two. At this rate, her face would sport a sunburn before she even made it to Texas. "I try, though I can't seem to find my rhythm with most of today's music—leaves me feeling like I have two left feet."

"So what kind of music transforms one foot back to normal?"

"You'll laugh." Her mother and sister always laughed. No doubt he would too.

He shook his head and held up three fingers. "Scout's honor, I won't."

She sighed, hoping this wouldn't be one of those moments you looked back on with regret. "I'm embarrassed to admit I've never really left the eighties when it comes to music. I blame my father."

His laughter, encouraging, not taunting, calmed like a sweet, soothing salve. "Always the man's fault."

"In this case, my mother's. She can be a bit unrelenting, so Dad made sure my sister and I were exposed to the lighter

narrowed in playful challenge. "They better make me walk on sunshine, mister."

CHAPTER FIVE

The flight attendant must've spiked his drink. There was no other explanation for why he'd ask this woman out on not one, but two dates less than thirty minutes after meeting her. She wasn't even his type. Long-legged, stacked, and no-strings-attached women made up his usual fare of dates. Women like Alana. Damn...Alana. She'd be madder than a bull in a room painted red if she learned he was in town and didn't call the moment the plane touched down. Fortunately, Alana was neither a fan of The Glass Cactus or history, so very little chance of running into her at either of his spontaneous dates with the jade-eyed beauty sitting next to him.

Her eyes.

They had to be the explanation for his unusual behavior. Her eyes had told him so much in the short time he'd known her —more than she realized. His military training finally provided him with a positive use. He'd been taught to study a person's eyes and expressions, or a hundred other emotional tells the face gave away, to learn if they were telling the truth or not. In her expressions, he saw a naïveté he was unaccustomed to seeing in the women he dated—if you wanted to call one-night stands dating. This woman both intrigued and perplexed him. Time to dig a little deeper. "So, how do you earn your paycheck, Melodie?"

Her surprised look at his question amused him and, dammit, melted another icicle around his heart. "Excuse me?"

"Let me rephrase the question. Where do you go to work each day? Your occupation?"

"Are you always this direct?"

He heard laughter. Had that been him? Not much laughter in his life lately. He shrugged. "The best way to get an answer. Besides," he softened his features, "if we get all of the preliminaries out of the way now, we can focus on the music and dancing later." Smooth must be his middle name.

"A children's librarian in a southwest suburb of Chicago." The words rushed out quickly as if she wasn't sure how he'd take the news.

"A what?"

"Big building, lots of books. Surely you've heard of such things?" Her eyes sparkled with amusement.

Dear God, he was definitely in trouble. Innocent wouldn't even scratch the surface of this woman.

Despite his best efforts to remain a gentleman, old habits die hard. "You're the sexiest librarian I've ever met."

"How many?"

The eyes he admired from the beginning turned accusing, another familiar expression. "How many what?" It didn't take a trained behavioral analyst to realize this conversation had taken a dramatic turn toward trouble.

"Librarians have you met?"

He searched his memory for an answer. "Umm, one or two when I was in school." *So deep in trouble...The air raid sirens are sounding loud and clear...run, seek cover!*

She shrugged and settled back, taking another sip of the vodka cranberry. "Then that wasn't much of a compliment."

Ouch. Score one for the librarian. A woman who had no trouble putting him in his place, something very few people had been successful with over the years. She'd done it in less than fifteen words. He liked this woman. "I'm sorry. I'll try harder next time, promise."

This time her shoulders lowered, and the shrug signaled defeat. "No apology necessary. Very few men bring their 'A' game once they learn they have a librarian on the hook."

"You don't have a very high opinion of yourself, do you?" Strong one moment and fragile the next. She was an emotional roller coaster taking him on one helluva ride.

"How do you earn your paycheck?" She retorted, apparently ignoring his assessment of her self-esteem.

"Former military." No details. None of her business. Sharing the details would send what was an already deteriorating conversation straight into the toilet.

"Well, solider, my opinions of myself and anything else personal in nature is on a need-to-know basis." She pierced him with those haunted pools of emerald one final time before turning her attention to the book she'd been holding in her lap since take off.

And I apparently don't need to know...

CHAPTER SIX

———

The rest of the flight passed uneventfully. Melodie escaped thirty thousand feet and the arrogant and irritatingly charming man sitting next to her by letting one of her favorite authors take her away to a time when Napoleon fought to gain world dominance, spies were everywhere, and men and women still held to the highest standards of manners.

A solider.

Former soldier. Didn't matter now anyway. Her hands gripped the armrests as they descended through the clouds, the turbulence making her wish she'd stuck with ginger ale rather than juice with alcohol. Slow, measured breaths. This was normal. Nothing to fear, according to the research. Simply the difference in air pressure above and below the clouds.

Words in a book often comforted her, giving her answers to many of life's questions. Words coming from other people— those were often disappointing and involved a great deal of second-guessing and doubt. She closed her eyes and focused on the hero in the novel, nothing like the enigma sitting next to her. One minute all Southern charm and manners, the next cocky ladies' man. The first intrigued her, the second—annoyed and unsettled.

"Eight o'clock work for you?"

The first words he'd spoken since she effectively tossed up a fresh row of barbed wire around the fragile woman desperate for protection from any further hurt. "I beg your pardon?"

"The Glass Cactus? Eighties music, walking on sunshine, remember?"

She studied him closely, trying to see if the gentleman was the one making the offer or the jerk. "You still want to go?"

"Look, I can't explain this. No more than you can, I bet. I enjoy your company—most of the time." He winked. "Life is short. No guarantees and all. I'd like to explore whatever this is. I'll meet you there so you won't have to worry about giving me your hotel name or anything."

His words sparked a brief memory of Tom. Life *was* short, too short. No promises for even tomorrow. And, as much as she hated to admit it, he was right. There was something. She didn't understand it, couldn't research it, and had no clue what would happen. She sensed a kindred spirit somewhere under the layers of bravado and overconfidence.

"What would your heroine do?"

The sincerity in his voice led her to believe the gentleman had control at the moment. "What?"

"In the book you've been reading since our first lovers' quarrel." The blue, iridescent eyes lightened even further with his teasing words.

Heat rose on Melodie's cheeks again like mercury in a thermometer on a hot July day. Honesty was always the best policy, right? "She would go."

"So, meet your hero for a fun evening of dancing. If you don't have a good time, he'll ride off into the sunset and never bother you again."

For some unknown reason, the thought of not seeing Daniel again disappointed her far more than she cared to admit. "Okay. Eight o'clock it is."

CHAPTER SEVEN

———

Daniel walked through the doorway promptly at eight. *Never early. Never late.* Beer, sweat, and women's perfume permeated his senses. *My kind of party.* He scanned the bar area looking for Melodie. Men in cowboy hats talking up women in high heels occupied most of the seats. Though there were some empty chairs, his date didn't seem to be the "I'll wait for you at the bar" type. Making his way through the hot bodies and large red couches interspersed for the comfort of the patrons who needed a rest from dancing in the lounge area, he searched the faces for a glimpse of her chocolate brown waves. Still no Melodie.

He rolled his neck to ease the growing tension. She didn't strike him as the type to agree to come and then back out. He moved to the center of the lounge area to check out the dancers. Though still early for a Friday night, the dance floor hosted a decent number of people gyrating to the band's rendition of a popular Def Leppard song.

Keen eyes scanned the crowd looking for her dark brown head bobbing in time to the music. Based on what he'd learned about her, it didn't seem likely she'd be hanging out with a bunch of strangers, but he felt compelled to cover all the bases. Still nothing. Where in the hell could she be? His disappointment seemed largely out of place for a woman he'd just met and had only known for a few hours. Time for a drink. Someday soon he'd have to find something besides alcohol and women to mask his pain, but that day was not today.

Moving back to the bar, he ordered a beer and made his way toward the outdoor patio. Maybe he could bum a cigarette off someone. He really didn't smoke, but sometimes he needed to distract himself from his nonstop internal diatribe.

Right before exiting, he caught sight of the brunette beauty, the most beautiful wallflower he'd ever laid eyes on. Melodie. In a denim skirt, white blouse, and red jacket—the picture of patriotism in a curvy, sexy package. He made eye contact and swaggered in her direction. "God bless the USA."

Her innocent look shot arousal through his veins, settling just below his belt. Thirty seconds and already he needed a cold shower. *Or a hot time in bed with Miss USA here.*

"Do you always make random comments, or do I just bring out the best in you?"

"You definitely bring out the best in me, sweetheart. I was just commenting about how patriotic you look in your red, white, and blue."

"Oh..." her blush matched her jacket.

Wanting to save her from herself, he gulped a few more swigs of his beer before tossing it in the trash can. "Let's dance, eighties girl."

Grabbing her hand, he pulled her away from the wall. His brows creased. She'd looked comfortable essentially fading into the woodwork. His eyes swept over her body. Why wouldn't she be the center of attention no matter what the occasion? Beautiful and smart with a hint of sweetness—a dangerous combination for his heart. Not wanting to delay his body in close proximity with hers one moment longer, he pulled her into the fray of the mosh pit, hoping modesty prompted her to lie about having two left feet. The moment her body started moving in time to the music, he forgot all about her feet as her softer curves begged for attention.

He matched his steps to hers. The crowd of people pressed against them, forcing their bodies closer. *This is more like it.* Muscles flexed, hips rotating—sharing all his best moves. Her moves were damn good too. Those hips...her breasts...even her legs...moving to Brian Adam's smooth beat. Each subtle sway sky-rocketed his libido to levels for which he couldn't be held responsible for very long.

The guitars strummed while the drums grew louder, feeding off the energy of the crowd. No slow songs from this group. Time to improvise and make his move. Pulling her tighter, he closed his eyes to focus on the warm-blooded woman fate had delivered in the seat next to him. This wallflower possessed curves which, at present, were exactly where he wanted them—pressed against his chest. Lower, the softness led to muscled thighs igniting multiple fantasies about them being wrapped around his hips. Despite his self-proclaimed promise to behave, he lowered his face to the curve of her neck, inhaling softly. Sweet Jesus, not only did she rally every ounce of testosterone in his body to attention, but her sweet smell was capable of bringing any man...this man...to his knees.

Dear God in heaven, he was in trouble.

* * *

"Daniel, please. Stop." Distance. Space. Time. Melodie needed all three right now as her head spun wildly out of control. His body against hers propelled the librarian in her straight to the erotic romance section of the bookshelf in her head. Not a safe place to be. Thinking became impossible, however, the moment his delectable lips touched the pulse point on her neck. Rivulets of pleasure slid through her nervous system, filling the pool of desire low in her abdomen.

Fortunately, the gentleman part of his dual personality heard her request and stepped away without pressing the point. "I'm sorry. I got carried away. You're so damn beautiful, I can't seem to help myself."

Between the accent and sincere expression, she wanted to believe there might be a grain of truth to his compliment. Nagging voices in the back of her head from her high school days taunted her. *Why can't you be more like Evelyn? Why can't you be successful like Evelyn? Why can't you find a husband like Evelyn?*

A lifetime in her sister's shadow prevented her from believing the veracity of his words. "You never mentioned you were blind. Now, are we going to stand here and try to have a conversation or dance? This is one of my favorite songs." Somewhere deep, she'd found some courage. Maybe people did change, maybe she could.

Bodies continued to move around them as the beginning strains of "Sweet Dreams" filled the dance floor. Her gaze held his, confusion dancing with desire in his sapphire depths. Finally, the cocky ladies' man veneer slipped over his face. "Hell yeah, we're going to dance."

CHAPTER EIGHT

———

Watching Melodie dance constituted equal parts heaven and hell. After a few songs, she seemed more relaxed and really having fun. He hated to admit it, but he was having fun too. *Been a long time...*

As the song ended, he pulled her off the dance floor. "You wore me out, woman. I deserve a drink. Your treat." Her buying him a drink would help compensate for shutting him down every time he tried to make a move on her.

His ego needed help to restore it to full capacity. For the first time in a long time, he'd offered sincere praise to a deserving woman, and what had she done? Ignored him and his compliment. Probably for the best anyway. Love 'em and leave 'em. His motto had been working for years. No need to change things now. *She's different. No denying it.*

She squeezed his hand and nodded. "You're on, cowboy."

They pushed their way up to the bar. Why did her sweat-slicked body smell so much better than the other people crowding around them? "A beer for me and a vodka cranberry for the lady." He held her tight, a possessive instinct. He wanted to be sure the other men knew tonight, she was with him.

"Let's go outside." With drinks in hand, he led her to the outside patio.

The giant kerosene heaters doubled as lamps and provided the perfect amount of lighting at night. A little privacy in a semi-crowded area.

He downed a few swigs of beer. "Cowboy?" His jeans tightened uncomfortably as her eyes swept over his attire.

"Blue jeans and cowboy boots—close enough for me."

"You for damn sure aren't from the south if I'm your idea of a cowboy. First off, no hat and no down-home, honest-to-goodness cowboy would be caught dead in this shirt."

Not enough cold water in Texas for the amount of showers he'd need to cool the fire she stoked when her manicured hand smoothed over his chest. "You're right, of course. I'll have to do additional research on proper cowboy attire. I'm glad you didn't go for a plaid button-down though. This T-shirt looks much nicer on you."

This woman might be the death of him. "You have a thing for research, don't you?" He needed to change the topic before he hiked up her skirt and had his way with her right there on the bar.

"Occupational hazard, I guess." Her hand continued its fiery path from his chest to his shoulder and then over his biceps. "You work out a lot?"

Deep breath in. Deep breath out. "Occupational hazard, I guess. Need to be fit to fight the bad guys, you know."

She smiled brightly, and his attempt at breathing stuttered worse than a nervous kid his first day of high school. "Touché." Her smile softened. "I had a wonderful time tonight. Thank you."

Despite the beer, his mouth went dry, and his heartbeat raced. He didn't want her to leave. Didn't want this night to end. Didn't want to miss the opportunity to touch her again—to kiss her. The beginning measures of another song filtered through the outdoor speakers. Finally, the eighties gods were with him as the DJ played the slow song he'd prayed for in the beginning—the love theme from *Footloose*. Could it get any better? "Dance with me before you go?"

Hesitation replaced her playfulness from a few moments ago. "I don't know."

Game time. He stepped a little closer, close enough for the sexual tension sizzling between them all evening to touch her, but not close enough to send his wallflower back into the paneling. "Consider it your patriotic duty for a cowboy who served his country."

His words prompted an immediate effect. Unfortunately, the opposite affect than he intended. Her face paled, and the life drained right out of those beautiful eyes. *What the hell?*

"I'm sorry. I can't. I have to go."

And with those apologetic words, his mysterious librarian left him standing alone at the patio railing. Oh yeah, the roller coaster this woman was taking him on was one helluva ride.

* * *

Air. She needed air. Memories of Tom surfaced along with the steep price of his patriotic duty. His service cost him his life and cost her a safe future. He might not have evoked the kind of intense reaction Daniel had since the first time their eyes met, but Tom offered her a security blanket, a plan B should she need one. He'd loved her for who she was and, most importantly, had never shown any interest in her big sister. Damn him for going and getting himself killed and upsetting the comfortable life they were going to create together.

She stumbled out of the bar toward her home away from home, grateful the location Daniel chose shared property with her hotel. This had all been a mistake, a big mistake. Hurried footsteps on the pavement behind her sent her pulse skyrocketing, the blood pounding in her ears until she could hear nothing else.

"Hey! Melodie! Stop! Please..."

The desperation in the "please" broke through the pounding, allowing guilt to weave itself inextricably into every nerve. Exhaling slowly, she turned to face him. "I'm sorry, truly. I'm just not...I can't...I..."

"Whoa, take it easy. Come here." He pulled her into his strong, comforting embrace.

Emotionally, she was in no position to fight him. Besides, she was tired of always being so damned independent, isolated, and introverted. Unwanted tears threatened, and she allowed Daniel's support. A part of her hated her weakness. Evelyn was always strong, and the goal she'd been given her entire life was to be more like Evelyn.

A few minutes later, her sense of calm found its way to the surface again. Pulling back from his embrace, she smiled. "Bet you've never had a date end like that before."

His hand cupped her cheek, robbing her of the ability to breathe. "I've never met a woman quite like you before."

She sniffled. "Is that a good or bad thing?"

Daniel shook his head and grinned. "Honestly? I'm not sure. Mostly good. Well, except when you ran out on me before that last dance. Was it something I said?"

The inability to speak followed her failure to breathe as his fingertips slipped through her hair, tucking errant strands behind her ear. He gently wiped away the remnants of the tears before the damp digits slipped across her lips.

She closed her eyes, searching for her voice. "It's complicated."

Soft lips on her forehead accelerated the rhythm of her heart, making its presence known. "I usually avoid complicated, but for you, I find myself willing to make an exception. How about you?"

"I usually do safe." Tom had been safe. Her books were safe. She preferred safe.

"And I don't feel safe to you?"

Melodie opened her eyes to take in the force of nature standing in front of her. His presence resembled a tornado, ripping into her life and uprooting all of her preconceived and decided-upon notions of what her life was to be—of the type of man she wanted to spend the rest of her life with. Just when the storm seemed out of control, she moved into the eye where an eerie calm and sense of peace prevailed—like now. "Not at all. But, I find myself willing to make an exception."

Her admission had apparently been enough for him. Adrenaline spiked from the strange mix of danger and excitement as his gorgeous face moved closer to hers. The storm infused her entire being as soft silk lips covered hers, endorphins releasing winds of pleasure. The tenderness brought peace and— need. She tried to deepen the kiss, but his hands on her cheeks held her motionless. With maddening slowness, he slid across her full lips to the corner. Phantom touches reached through the surface and delved deep into her wounded heart to deliver life-giving energy to the half-dead organ. Over and over, he kissed her without quite kissing her.

Finally, she could take no more. "Please, Daniel…" Her voice a soft whisper in the still night.

His hands slid down the column of her throat and over her arms, pulling her body flush with his as his tongue slid across her highly sensitized mouth. Parting her lips farther, their connection deepened.

She angled her head to participate in the kiss. *Sweet Lord in heaven. I've been missing out. So good and oh so dangerous.*

Endless swirls of desire licked at her arousal lifting her need to unbearable levels. Breathless, she broke the connection. "When will I see you again?"

Though still in a bit of a daze from the intensity of the kiss, she couldn't help but notice the strong features on his face turn conflicted for a few moments. Age-old uncertainty set in again. Had he not enjoyed the kiss as she had? The conflict disappeared, replaced by cockiness. She almost hated to hear what would come out of those sensuous lips next.

"Does that mean you aren't inviting me back to your room tonight?"

So one kiss and he expected her to spend the night with him? They barely knew each other! Aggravated, she pulled away from his grasp. "I guess your normal date would be grateful for the invitation, but I'm going to pass. Thanks for the evening, Daniel. It's been illuminating." She took a few steps and then turned for one final glance. "Have a great life. I hope you find what you're looking for and it lasts more than one night."

The centrifugal force of her emotions made it difficult to stay on course, but years of adamant independence and fighting with her mother paid off with staunch internal reserve. Tonight taught her a valuable lesson. A storm chaser she was not.

CHAPTER NINE

_____

Sunday

Dry mouth. Pounding headache. Churning stomach. Daniel couldn't remember the last time he'd had a hangover, and this was the mother of all hangovers. After that damn kiss, the need for his beautiful, sexy, reserved librarian burned hotter than the San Antonio sun in July. He'd pulled out all his best moves and let the gentleman inside of him come out to play last night. What had been his reward for being compassionate, caring, and tender? A total eclipse of the sun followed by an arctic gale from the most infuriating woman he'd ever met. Why the hell did he even care? God knows she wasn't the first woman to turn him down, though, admittedly, there hadn't been many, especially not after a soul-searing kiss like the one they shared.

Love 'em and leave 'em. That was his motto, his standard operating procedure, his SOP. It aggravated him beyond measure his SOP wasn't working, wasn't what he wanted, this time. _Damn that woman._

He'd drowned the fires of his passion with cheap beer and the occasional shot of Jägermeister. Well, maybe more than the occasional shot. To make matters worse? Though the details were fuzzy, he knew at least two separate women offered to console him in a very physical way. Did he go with them? No. Did he call Alana to share he was in town and in need of the kind of attention only she could give? No. Did he consume alcohol until the sole remaining rational thought prompted him to call a taxi to take him back to his hotel? Hell yes!

Now he was paying the price with the Army Drum and Bugle Corps conducting drills in the space between his throbbing temples. *Damn that woman!*

Coffee, aspirin, and a hot shower eased the pounding somewhat, allowing him to devise a strategy. Just walk away. Definitely the course of action he should take. Get off the roller coaster ride this innocent, emerald-eyed vixen strapped him into from the first moment her body touched his. Yes, that was what he should do.

He topped off his coffee and stared out the hotel window. The bleak parking lot view held little appeal and currently mirrored his life. Empty. Flat. Hard. Except when he was with Melodie. Her desperate kiss cut through the bullshit and hinted at the promise of the woman he could take home to his parents. Someone he could hold at night.

He sighed. He knew what he *should* do. He also knew, without a doubt, what he was going to do. *Damn that woman.*

* * *

Insufferable. The best word to describe the man who'd been a constant source of annoyance since the moment they met—less than twenty-four hours ago. Melodie tossed and turned all night, reliving his kiss. Pleasure. Annoyance. Guilt. Tom's kisses had been nice, a soft rain filling her body with slow-rising pleasure. Daniel's kisses were more like a tsunami of sensation drowning her in sensory overload. The two didn't compare. Of course, Tom never treated her as a single-use container to be thrown away after just one night.

Tom.

As his name whispered across her lips, she knew the look he'd be giving her right now if he were here. He'd been so good at pushing, yet accepting. Even when she'd proposed the marriage pact, he'd chuckled and agreed, all the while assuring her she'd find Mr. Right long before the deadline.

A wave of sadness washed over her already tired body. Not only had Tom been wrong, but her best friend had left her to deal with her life and her family all on her own. Damn him and the war that killed him.

Her phone buzzed. A quick glance at the caller ID sent her headache up another notch. "Hey, Ev."

"How you doing, kiddo?"

Melodie bristled at the childhood nickname her sister still insisted on calling her. "As well as can be expected. Just trying to get away from it all for a bit."

"I'm worried about you. You can't run away from your problems."

Says the woman who has no problems. "Well, thanks for the concern, big sis, but actually, I can." After the emotional evening with Daniel and the hurt still present from losing Tom, she'd endured all the well-meaning platitudes and advice she could take.

"Look, come home. There's an associate in my firm who's perfect for you."

Melodie closed her eyes. Just what she needed. A blind date. Ugh! Why couldn't everyone leave her alone? Exhaling slowly, she tried one last stab at diplomacy before the conversation moved to the slippery slope of family angst and drama. "I appreciate the gesture, but I'm still grieving Tom. I'm not ready for a blind date."

This time her sister's exasperated sigh filled the connection. "I know you two were close and devised this crazy agreement to marry when you turned thirty if no better options presented themselves, but the simple fact you even considered such an agreement demonstrates your need for help in this area. Honestly, Mel. Tom was a nice guy, but you only considered a future with him because he was away most of the time. He was safe. You didn't love him…not like a woman should love her future husband. It's time to move out of your fantasy world, and get on with your life. You need to come home."

Enough! Her family treated her like she was a child who couldn't make a decision for herself if her life, or her future, depended on it. "Last time I checked, I was over twenty-one— way over twenty-one. I can do anything I damn well please and choose to be with whomever I want, whether you approve or not."

"Well, at least one thing hasn't changed. You're as stubborn as ever. Someday, Mel, you'll realize I only have your best interest at heart."

The tears made their afternoon matinee appearance. This long-running waterworks show needed to retire. "Maybe someday, Ev, you'll realize my idea of my best interest and yours aren't even close."

"Do whatever you want…you always do anyway."

The silence from the disconnected line echoed loudly throughout the room. Melodie curled up on the bed, pulling the pillow close to her body, as the moisture continued to escape from her eyes. Thoughts of Tom filled her aching head. She missed him like she'd miss any friend taken in the prime of their life. Did she love him? No. Love hadn't really been the point though. She was comfortable with him. He had been her best friend. She pounded the pillow a few times for effect. God, she hated it when Evelyn was right.

CHAPTER TEN

―――――

Daniel paced the length of the telephone cord in his room as he waited for her to answer the phone. After several, heart-stopping rings, he heard the warm, soothing tones of her voice. "Hello."

"Hey, Melodie, it's Daniel."

"What? How did you find me?"

I've got skills. Not wanting her to think he was a stalker, he chuckled. "I wish I could take credit for being a super sleuth, but you introduced yourself to me on the plane, which provided your first and last name. When you ran away last night, it wasn't hard to figure out where you were staying. I also know you didn't get a rental car at the airport, which narrowed the options to the hotel on the same property as the bar as your home away from home."

There was a significant pause. "Sounds like stalking to me, and I didn't run away. What do you want?"

No, you stumbled, desperate to get away from me. "To prove I'm not a total jerk—"

"Not a total jerk. More like Dr. Jekyll and Mr. Hyde. One I really like and want to get to know more, the other..."

"The other is a jerk." No sense denying the truth.

Her smile almost came through the phone. "I was going to say arrogant jerk, but we'll leave it at jerk."

Go time. Damn, this woman intrigued him as no one else had. "Let me prove I'm more Jekyll than Hyde. Have dinner with me tonight."

Another pause. This woman could be responsible for giving him a heart attack at a young age.

"You have one more chance to prove it to me. If Mr. Hyde so much as shows his face tonight, our date with history will never happen."

"You won't be sorry, Melodie. I'll pick you up at five."

He cut the connection, not wanting to give the arrogant jerk part of his personality a chance to say something that would make her change her mind. He rubbed the back of his neck in an effort to ease the tension. Her parting words last night rang in his ears. He hoped he found what he was looking for soon too. He wasn't sure how much more his wounded heart could withstand, and all of the Band-Aids he'd been using to mask the pain were no longer working.

Daniel spotted her before she saw him. God, she was beautiful. Black pants and a dark green sweater. Though not a romantic, he'd heard enough woman-talk to know the color would make her eyes sparkle like jewels in the moonlight.

Maybe a little romantic. Must be the librarian. "Hey, Beautiful."

Her face lit up even as she shook her head, a subtle denial again of his compliment. Regardless, her smile sent a lightning bolt straight to his groin. He wanted this woman— badly.

"Hey, yourself."

Wanting to show he was capable of being a gentleman, he extended his arm to escort her away from the sprawling complex comprising the grounds of her hotel. "Milady," he smiled.

"Are you playing the role of my knight in shining armor tonight?" She laughed as she slipped her hand in the crook of his arm.

"I can make tonight a fairy tale for you, if that's what you want. Although, I may not be as smooth and gallant as the heroes in your books, but I'll do my damnedest to show you a good time."

A look of—was it guilt?—crossed her face. "There's a reason they call it fiction. Life never works out as perfectly as it does in the books."

He opened the door of the Mustang convertible for her and tried not to focus on her long legs or the strappy black sandals showing off sexy, red toenails. "Is that why you read them?"

Quickly closing the door, he strutted around the front of the car. *Might as well give her a look at one of my best assets.* Sliding in beside her, he brought the engine to life. Something about powerful engines appealed to him. Fast. Dangerous. Loud. Similar to the way he'd lived his life—until recently. He missed his motorcycle back home. Images of Melodie in black leather, straddling his cherry red Ducati, did absolutely nothing to ease the fire burning behind the zipper of his Levis.

"I suppose."

Her softly spoken words dragged him reluctantly out of the fantasy and back to reality. "You suppose what?"

Dark eyebrows creased on her face, adding to the charm of her confusion. "You asked me if I read books because they worked out better than real life. I was answering."

He shifted the car smoothly into gear. "Real life definitely bites sometimes, doesn't it?"

"Definitely." The innocent statement prompted the faraway look on her face again.

Damn, he needed to understand what was going on inside that beautiful head of hers. He didn't want to screw things up before they even started. And, God help him, for once—he didn't want to screw things up. Time to unleash the full gentleman on her.

"All right. Try this compliment on for size. I've never met someone, librarian or otherwise, with eyes as beautiful as yours. They would give emeralds a run for their money in a contest for stunning."

As he hoped, the subject of his compliment, those dazzling eyes, focused on him and, thank God above, they were at a stoplight, so he could return the intensity of her gaze. She offered a slight nod. "Your compliment would give any romance book hero a run for his money."

"Score one for Doctor Jekyll."

Her laughter filled the air, and he couldn't help but smile too. He sent an urgent message to his lower half. The agenda for tonight was different. No bag 'em and tag 'em on this outing. No, the objective for tonight consisted of more laughter and smiles from the beautiful woman sitting next to him. While the head below his belt absorbed the mandate, the one resting above his shoulders realized he wanted more than one night with this woman...definitely more.

"Jekyll–one. Hyde–zero. So far so good. Five minutes down, hours to go." Melodie teased.

*Hours to go...*Daniel liked the sound of a long night ahead of him. "So, for my next impressive move, I've selected Mi Casa as our dinner choice. You like Mexican food, right?"

"Does Taco Bell count?"

He grinned but cut her a quick look. "We're talking authentic Mexican here. If you're still craving one of those Dorito tacos after dinner, I'll run thru the drive-thru on the way back to your hotel."

"I'm willing to try." She looked out the window, squinting into the bright sun. "Seems a shame to have a convertible in this unrelenting heat. You wouldn't get to put the top down very often, I bet."

His overactive imagination promptly offered up images of Melodie's hair blowing freely in the wind, her expression smiling and uninhibited. He stopped the fantasy short of imagining her spread out on the hood, crying out his name in pleasure. Yeah, he might as well invite Mr. Hyde in for dinner if those illicit thoughts were allowed free rein. "If we take our time at dinner, the sun will set, and the temperature will drop to a bearable level. Then we can put the top down on the way home if you want."

A beautiful mix of happiness, excitement and shyness filled out her complexion. "I'd like that. Thank you."

Score two for Dr. Jekyll...at least one and a half.

A few minutes later, Daniel turned in to the parking lot. A brown building with the name of the restaurant in bold red letters sat prominently in the middle of the lot.

Melodie surveyed the exterior, unique décor of the restaurant. Chalk drawings of different scenes, including guitar players with sombreros, children playing soccer in the streets with brightly colored shirts, and the bold red, white, and green of the Mexican flag. Each drawing offering a colorful panorama of a slice of life in Mexico. "How extraordinary."

Daniel opened her door and extended his hand to help her up. Either accidently or on purpose, he pulled a little too hard, causing her to fall onto him again, reminiscent of their encounter on the airplane. This time, though, his arm circled her waist and steadied her soft frame against his. "I'd say we should stop meeting like this, but I kinda like it."

"You don't hear me complaining, do you?" Her softness pressed into his body, searing everywhere they touched with a heat stronger than the Texas sun at noon. This woman had no idea the affect she had on red-blooded males.

This red-blooded male in particular.

"Me neither, but we should probably get inside before they give away our reservations and," he let his hand slip a little lower until the small of her back rested under his palm, "before you tempt Mr. Hyde out of the dark corner I've relegated him to as punishment for misbehaving yesterday."

She stepped away, giving them both some space. "Good idea." She kissed him gently on the cheek. Leaving her hand in his, she pulled him toward the door.

He followed, like a lamb to the slaughter, knowing without a doubt his life would never be the same after spending time with this enchanting woman.

CHAPTER ELEVEN

———

Impressive. Not only had Daniel been a perfect gentleman thus far, but the restaurant he selected for their dinner was nothing short of amazing. Besides the stunning yet simple beauty of the exterior, the cool, dark interior of the restaurant boasted bright colorful blankets, pictures, pottery and other authentic Hispanic decorations. The food was also a little slice of Spanish heaven. "I love when they serve the chips warm."

"The only way. Don't be a wuss. Try some of the salsa *verde*. I bet you like it hot."

He was flirting—flirting with danger even, but she couldn't resist. "I don't mind a little heat on my lips."

Daniel's eyes rolled back into his head as he groaned. "Damn it, woman, who's being bad now?"

She lowered her lashes and smiled. "Sorry. You're right. You've been on your best behavior. I should do the same."

Despite his arrogance and views toward women, his sincere compliments and effort to spend time with her had unlocked something deep within her heart. She'd been cautious for so long—fear of history repeating itself. Tonight was about the new beginning she'd promised herself. She only hoped she'd be able to see this through and not run, either physically or metaphorically, from the challenge and opportunity this man presented.

"Shall we try the getting to know more about you conversation again?"

His eyes flashed. This was one of those times the ability to read people better would help her understand what the look in his eyes meant. Making a mental note, she assigned herself the task of finding books on nonverbal communication and reading up on the subject when she got home. If the goal was to start living her life outside the pages of books, knowing how to read people would serve her well in the venture.

"What do you want to know?" She looked into his eyes, searching for some clue. Was he making an effort for her? From the little she did understand about people, it appeared that way. At least she hoped so. The gesture warmed her more than the salsa *verde*.

She waited while the food was placed in front of them and sampled her first taste of the enchilada. The combination of flavors, savory tinged with heat, tantalized her taste buds. "Oh, this is amazing. Another point scored for Dr. Jekyll."

He gave a slight smile. "I also get a point for not kissing you senseless in the parking lot earlier."

A quick sip of the strawberry margarita in the large glass proved a useless attempt to hide the heat spreading across her cheeks. "Maybe two." *Subtract two, that is. The man could kiss. Dear God, could he kiss.* Time to get the conversation back on track. "You said you were former military. What branch?"

His shoulders moved back as his chin thrust out. "Army, one hundred and first airborne division."

She sat up straighter and smiled. "That was the same division my dad served with in Vietnam. Screaming Eagles."

"Hooah."

Laughter bubbled to the surface as she remembered all the reminders her father had given her growing up about not confusing the different branches of the military. "Yes, not to be mistaken for hoorah."

He widened his eyes before giving her a big smile. "Hell no. We don't allow marine talk around here. Do we soldier?"

The laughter escaped, and she shook her head. "Sir, no, sir."

After a few more bites of food, the desire to know more about him prompted another question. "What do you do now?"

"That's not an easy question." Daniel's attention diverted to his beer bottle.

Remembering his words to her on the plane, she grinned and winked. "I believe you phrased it best. How do you earn your paycheck?"

He played with the label on the bottle, his eyes lowered. "I don't currently earn one. I'm going into business for myself."

"What type of business?"

Finally, eye contact. "Repairing and building custom motorcycles. I love to ride and tinker around with them. Figured after doing what Uncle Sam wanted, followed closely by what my ex wanted, it was time to do what I wanted."

"Good for you." She reached across the table and laid her hand over his, squeezing it in encouragement. "Tell me about your ex." There was no true explanation for her question other than her continued curiosity about what made the man sitting across from her tick. He intrigued her. She was beginning to think she liked intrigue.

"Most women don't like to hear about the past women in a man's life."

"Well, you said she was your ex. You're not still sleeping with her, are you?" If he answered yes, she would perform her vanishing act faster than she did last night. She prayed her purse contained enough cash for a cab ride back to the hotel.

Daniel's face screwed up in a look resembling horror. "God, no."

"That bad, eh?"

He nodded. "That bad. What about you? Ever been married?"

She lifted her hand to her hair and slowly twisted a lock. *Don't cry. He doesn't know. It's an innocent question. "*No, never."

"So no kids then?"

Her heart clenched along with her jaw. *Honestly, get a grip.* She knew it was irrational, but this topic always unsettled her. "No. You?"

Unlike the forced smile she put on for others when this topic arose, Daniel's smile lit up his entire face. "My daughter is the best thing that has ever happened to me, and the only good thing that came from my relationship with my ex. As a matter of fact, the only reason I still talk to the ex is Annie. Have to keep the peace or she'll use my visitations with her as a bargaining chip."

He has a daughter..."Tell me about her."

"The ex?"

"No, I've changed my mind. I'd rather hear about Annie."

"Does the fact I have a daughter scare you off? I wouldn't blame you if it did."

No, but the fact he might want more children gave her pause. *Let it go.* "I'm a children's librarian, remember? I adore kids."

"Anastasia is eight. Everyone calls her Annie. Her nickname is Princess. Blonde hair and blue eyes like her mother, but that's where the likeness stops. She's sweet, full of happiness, and not jaded by life. Her smile, hugs, and the way she calls me Daddy make me believe in second chances. She's the only female I've met and known for more than a couple days who hasn't screwed me over. Well, so far anyway."

"Am I the only female you've encountered who didn't take the offer of a one-night stand?" Her words were meant to gently tease, but the moment his eyes hardened, and the warmth of his hand in hers left, she knew she'd failed. Her damned curiosity, but she'd needed to know. She might be willing to try a new path in life, but she wasn't a one-night stand kind of girl.

"You don't understand." His fingers ran through his short blond hair.

He was right. She didn't understand. God help her, she wanted to. "Look, I'm not good at reading people. Reading books is more my thing. However, you broadcast your opinions about relationships and women loud and clear. Even a naïve children's librarian can pick up on that little tidbit."

Another swallow of beer before he slowly exhaled and shrugged. "Survival instinct. Cause and effect."

Her heartbeat increased. Cause and effect she understood, but she needed the details. "You've lost me again."

"In the service, we're taught to pay attention to our surroundings and react accordingly. You trust those who are on your side and react to any threats with any means necessary to survive."

Thoughts of Tom and the trust he'd given to those allegedly on his side slipped unbidden to the front of her thoughts. He'd been given no opportunity to react, no opportunity to survive. Fighting back sadness and anger, she refocused on Daniel. "Sounds reasonable."

He pushed his plate to the center of the table. "Reasonable except I didn't realize when I got home from each tour, women would prove to be the real threats. They all wanted something from me—usually money, sex, and the list went on and on. Problem was, none of them wanted to give me what I wanted."

Daniel now had her undivided attention. What did a man like this want? "Which was?"

"Someone to share my life. Someone to cuddle with at night. Someone who wouldn't take my heart and treat it like a piece of rental property and only kept it around as long as it generated income."

Words failed her. How did one respond to such a statement? Fortunately, or unfortunately, depending on how she looked at it, he'd saved her from responding.

"So, after getting screwed over repeatedly by women, I switched to survival mode. They used me, so I used them—cause and effect."

Her appetite vanished with the lighthearted banter they'd been sharing throughout most of the evening. She'd wanted to know, and now she was at a loss to respond. "I'm so sorry."

The warmth of his hand returned, along with gentle pressure. "Here's the thing, I don't feel that way around you. Like I said when we first met, I can't explain this, but I sure as hell want to explore wherever this takes us. I haven't been down this road in a long time. Kind of makes me feel like I'm on an adventure."

His shy, gorgeous, ice-melting smile beamed straight into her heart, turning her insides into the equivalent of overcooked oatmeal.

He could switch gears much quicker than she. Time to engage the deflection defenses and regroup. "At least you've had adventures. My idea of wild and crazy is a spy thriller with a steamy romance."

Hurt flashed across his face. "This trip, these last couple of days...don't they count as an adventure?"

The wildest adventure of my life to date. "Of course. I've never felt so—alive. Just as I only know Survival-mode Daniel, you've only met the newly christened Adventure Melodie, currently starring in her debut movie." Another sip finished off the sweet, frozen mug of liquid courage sitting in front of her. "As I'm sure you've guessed, I spend a lot of time with my nose in a book. Life makes more sense in the stories. The plots are well-thought-out, the hero always gets the girl in the end, good prevails, and evil pays. I like the nice neat bow tied around each one. As you've alluded, life…Well, life just doesn't happen that way."

"Can I ask you a personal question?" The soft, calming tone of his voice reminded her of how she addressed the children.

"As long as I don't have to promise to answer."

He chuckled and lifted her hand to those satiny lips, placing a tender kiss to the back.

Oh hell, now I'll answer, whether I want to or not.

"Why haven't you had any adventures?"

She closed her eyes to prevent him from seeing the pain of a childhood living in perfection's shadow. "Cause and effect."

"My turn not to follow."

He'd shared. It was her turn to explain. "Sibling rivalry at its finest. My older sister has been the proverbial golden child from the moment she entered the world with, and I quote, the easiest labor a woman ever endured."

"Ouch. Let me guess, your entry into the world was…"

"Long, painful and, of course, breech." Melodie couldn't help but laugh as she pictured her mother's dramatic face every time she told the story.

"That covers the first day of life. From what I can see, you turned out stunningly beautiful, self-sufficient, and smart."

She shrugged her shoulders, unsure how to make him understand. "No matter what I did, it was never good enough— never ambitious enough—never 'Evelyn' enough."

"Evelyn enough?"

A rueful smile, "My older sister. Valedictorian. Homecoming queen. Married the all-American quarterback. Delivered two equally beautiful grandchildren. And, lest we forget, the youngest woman at her firm to make partner. Need I go on?"

"Damn."

"Exactly. I couldn't, didn't want to, compete with such perfection. Every guy who showed an interest in me during high school only did so to get close to my sister. So, I stopped dating and started reading." *Except for Tom.* "By the time college rolled around, the stories in my books were far more interesting than any of my interactions with real people. Much to my mother's disappointment and aggravation, I switched my major from accounting to library science."

"Books are to you like gold is to King Midas."

She nodded. "There's a treasure trove of information contained between the bindings. I love researching and discovering new details about life."

"Just not living it."

Well, he certainly knew how to read her. Of course, she wasn't all that complicated. She couldn't decide if the notion relieved or worried her. "No." She thought back to her days in the dorm. "I've never even stayed out all night before. How sad is that? It should be a rite of passage in college, shouldn't it?"

Daniel's face lit up, dispelling some of the gloom surrounding their table. He signaled their waitress for the check. "Fortunately for you, makeup tests are available for those situations."

His enthusiasm prompted excitement and a rapid pulse even if his words left her clueless. "And you've lost me again."

"Let's get outta here. We'll put the top down and cruise over to Lake Ray Hubbard. We'll watch the sun set, then hit the open road again and see where we end up. Before you object, I promise Dr. Jekyll will be the one driving. I'll put Mr. Hyde in the trunk." He winked. "Well, unless you invite him to the party."

She wanted to. It sounded like so much fun. "I don't know."

"You got somewhere else to be?"

Melodie opened her mouth to answer. She had absolutely nowhere else to be. No job to go to in the morning.

No boyfriend waiting. No commitments. "Nowhere." Honesty was still the best policy, right?

"Then come on. Let's do this." He reminded her of little Johnny Stephens when he begged her to read a story "Just one more time, Ms. Melodie." She'd never been able to refuse Johnny, and, so far, her record remained the same for the handsome man sitting across the table.

"All right. You talked me into it." Not that she'd put up much of a fight. She needed to find a way to take back some control. Being out of control never proved a positive aspect in her life. Not even Daniel's charm would change that.

As they walked toward the car, Melodie heard Evelyn's golden voice nagging in her ear. "Great idea, kiddo. Get in a car with a guy you just met, you barely know, and let him drive you to God knows where. I hope we can find your body."

God, she hoped Evelyn wasn't right…this time.

CHAPTER TWELVE

———

Heaven. Of all the places he'd been in the world, and he'd been to many, nothing compared with watching Melodie's face as the sun set over the lake. Her hair, a blanket of silk resting above her shoulders, now framed her face in wild, sexy disarray from the ride over. Her countenance registered pure bliss from the first moment the wind started whipping around her face.

First time I've put that look on a woman's face and not been naked.

She looked free, happy even. God help him, he wanted to be responsible for putting that look on her face every day and a look of need every night.

The sky was a beautiful medley of purple and oranges as the sun prepared to skim the water before disappearing for the night. A final streak of yellow, the last remnants of the sun's rays coloring the blue lake, stretched out over the water, almost touching the land.

"So breathtakingly beautiful." Melodie turned toward him. "Thank you for talking me into coming here."

He couldn't stop himself. His hand smoothed wisps of hair from her cheek, tucking them behind her ear. "You're breathtakingly beautiful."

Forcing himself to move slowly, he leaned toward her. He wanted to savor every detail of this moment. First, he kissed her temple focusing on the soft-as-silk hair. One more kiss there before anointing her forehead with the same deliberate attention. He respected her mind almost as much as he did her body. Cheeks, reddened from the hot Texas sun, warmed his lips before he moved to his final destination. Their lips touched.

Absent the intensity from last night, warmth infused Daniel—like a pitcher being filled by a slow-running faucet, controlled and satisfying. Plenty of night left. No need to rush and scare her off again. He pulled away and kissed her gingerly on the tip of her nose. The warmth continued as she smiled, taking his hand before resuming her watch of the vanishing sunset. Though he wanted to only watch her, he forced himself to focus on the natural beauty in front of him.

Fifteen minutes later, he squeezed her hand. "Ready to hit the open road?"

"Oh yes."

Was it possible for her eyes to light up brighter than the setting sun? Not even the most amazing sunset could tear him away from staring into her green, fathomless depths of light. *Maybe I'm a hopeless romantic. Damn. Forty-eight hours with this woman and I've gone all soft.* "Then let's not waste a single second."

"You're crazy!" Melodie called out over the wind whipping around her face.

"Crazy about you." He pushed the gas pedal a little harder to increase their current speed. Not another living soul or automobile could be found on Interstate 281 this time of night. His need for speed and Melodie's constant smile, as she stared up at the moon hanging brightly in the sky, represented the main explanation for his lead foot tonight. A run-in with a State Trooper wouldn't even dampen his mood right now. He'd gladly pay any ticket for the fun life had delivered over the past few hours.

"Where are we going?"

"San Antonio. We'll take a walk along the River Walk, find a late night diner to grab a quick bite, and then head back to Dallas. Should arrive in time to watch the sunrise. Sound good?"

"Sounds amazing."

Her unbridled joy washed over his war-hardened heart, bringing a sense of contentment. Other than honesty and respect, she'd asked nothing of him. Hell, she even paid for a round of drinks last night. He needed to be careful, or he'd lose himself in the worst kind of way in this woman. A way that meant he could never go back to the jaded man he'd become. Four hours later, Daniel pulled off the highway and took an incline ramp before turning into a "Share the Ride" parking lot. Lifting the hand Melodie still held, he kissed hers gently. "Ready to bring in the morning?"

"I'll grab the coffee." She retrieved the two cups of Starbucks, extra-hot, they'd procured a couple exits back, along with some cinnamon scones.

Daniel hurried to the passenger side and opened the door for her. "Your sunrise awaits, milady."

"Where do you want to sit?" Melodie surveyed the limited options.

Daniel opened the trunk and pulled out a blanket. He grinned as Melodie's eyes widened when he threw the blanket across the hood of the car. "C'mon. Best seat in the house."

"Seriously?"

He nodded. "Seriously. Have I led you astray since our little adventure started yesterday evening?"

Grinning, she handed him his coffee and the bag of scones and crawled up on the hood. Her first attempt almost landed her on the ground as she, along with the blanket, slid down the vehicle. "Oh!" Somehow, she managed to not spill the entire contents of her coffee.

He tossed his coffee and the scones to the ground and caught her just in time to stop her fall straight to the asphalt. Making sure she had her feet under her, he picked the blanket up and repositioned it on the hood. "Let's try this again." This time, he scooped her into his arms, holding her close enough to enjoy the lingering scent of her perfume.

"You really have to stop saving me." Melodie whispered, her body sliding close to his as they settled in for the sunrise.

"I've saved countless people over the course of my life but none I've enjoyed more than you. Besides," he placed a soft kiss on her temple, "you don't need saving. You're a strong woman capable of taking care of yourself." Though true, a tug of protectiveness surged from deep inside. She might not need him to take care of her, but he wouldn't mind doing so.

The bright rays of the sun peeked over the horizon, filling the darkness with radiating light, waking the world to another beautiful day. "Thank you for helping me ace this makeup test. Not only was it my first time to stay out all night, I can't imagine a better evening, and the morning is shaping up quite nicely."

A buzzing noise broke into the perfection of their moment. Daniel needed only one guess to know who'd be calling him this early. He reached into his pocket to hit the ignore button.

"Do you need to get that? It's gone off several times over the last few hours."

"Nothing that can't wait until morning officially arrives. Now be quiet and share your coffee, since mine is watering the grass right now." Life was about to get very complicated…again. He wanted to enjoy these last few moments with Melodie. This time the annoying tug begged him to not screw this up.

"You take yours with cream and sugar?" Melodie handed him the cup. Her eyes focused on his mouth as he took a sip.

His face scrunched as he handed the beverage back to her. "Geez, woman. I like sweet, but your coffee could send a man into a diabetic coma."

He sure as hell didn't need coffee with Melodie sitting right next to him. He pulled her into his arms, searing her lips with a kiss. The cup slipped from her hand, joining his on the ground below. His ego soared. She didn't need coffee either. His tongue swept across her mouth, and she opened to invite him in. Damn. Melt-in-your-mouth sweetness washed over his taste buds, turning his craving for her into an all-encompassing addiction. If he didn't get his fix soon…

Nerve endings fired and his heart pounded violently in his chest. His sexy wallflower—a convertible Mustang—sunrise—kisses for caffeine. Didn't get any better than this.

Breaking the kiss, she sat up. The sharp inhale of her breath said the kiss had affected her too. "Now neither of us has any coffee."

Not exactly the comment he expected after a mind-blowing kiss. He ran his hands over his face and through his short-cropped hair. "With you in my bed, I'd give up coffee, caffeine, sugar—the list goes on."

"We should get back. You have to take care of your persistent caller, and I need some sleep."

Unsure why the quick need for distance, Daniel slid off the car and turned to face her. He opened his mouth to ply her with a smart-ass comment but, remembering his promise Mr. Hyde would stay locked in the trunk, he stifled the urge. "If that's what you want. Can I see you again later today? You promised to come to the JFK Memorial with me."

Her face, bathed in the soft morning light, turned conflicted and indecisive. If this woman turned him down after he'd been on his best behavior...

"Yes, I did. Pick me up around three?"

He shook his head. "Six. You'll want to see the memorial in the evening when they turn the lights on. Mesmerizing is the only word I can think of to describe the sight."

"Alright, six it is then." She hesitated before sliding off the car and turning to face him. "Thank you again for the wonderful time."

His phone buzzed again. He knew who it was. No point in looking. He'd call her as soon as he dropped Melodie off and try to talk his way out of the hornet's nest Alana would surround him with as soon as she discovered the truth. And she would discover it because he'd tell her. After spending time with Melodie, time with Alana wasn't going to cut it anymore. Not that it ever did.

"You really should respond to whoever's trying to reach you. What if it's your daughter?"

"It's not."

"Family?"

"No." This woman was relentless, and if she didn't stop, their adventure would end in a fight. *Please, woman, let it go.*

"Then it must be the ex. Otherwise, why would you be so evasive."

"Are you always this nosey?" He touched the tip of her nose with his finger. "You do have a very cute nose though." Misdirection—worth a shot.

She shrugged. "I'm curious by nature."

As if he hadn't picked up on that from almost hour one. "How about if I promise to fill you in over dinner tonight after we finish up at the memorial?" What the hell was wrong with him? Offering the truth about Alana? Closet masochist? No, something much more disturbing. Melodie made him want to be a better man, as cliché as that sounded. He'd break things off with Alana, come clean with Melodie, then pray she still wanted to continue their relationship or whatever in the hell this was called. *Sexually frustrating comes to mind.*

"Am I going to want to hear this?"

He cupped her face with his hands and pulled her into a tender kiss. "I keep telling you I want to explore whatever this is. In order to continue our..." He smoothed his hand down the gentle curve of her neck before stopping over her frantically beating heart, "exploration, I need you to understand who I am."

She pulled him into another kiss, this one more intense.

Forgetting about Alana, he immersed himself in their connection. Hot, sweet, and sexy as hell. He wanted and needed more of this woman, wanted to taste her and needed to alleviate some of the sexual tension and frustration that had been his constant companion since their first dance. Hell, maybe even before. Sweeping his tongue across her lips, he tasted the slightest hint of cream and sugar. When her lips parted slightly, he deepened the kiss, letting his tongue scrape across her teeth. He moaned, well, a combination of a moan and a growl. God, this was good. Damn good. Honestly, if he didn't have this woman soon...

He pulled away, "If you don't plan on inviting me back to your room, then we need to stop."

"I...I'm sorry."

Damn, infuriating woman. He lowered his head to claim her in another fiery kiss. When her hands slid up his arms and around his neck to pull their bodies closer, Mr. Hyde broke the lock on the trunk and joined the party. He slid one hand into the tangled waves of her hair and the other to the curve of her bottom, holding her hard against him. She'd realize instantly how far gone he already was—how much he'd been holding back. He tore his mouth away, desire to take her to bed consuming every nerve ending in his body. "Don't be sorry, baby, just don't say good-bye yet."

Her face showed conflict and indecision. He stretched in order to keep his hands busy and from touching her as she made her decision.

I should win an award for being such a damn gentleman. The phone in his pocket buzzed again, breaking the spell.

"We have to say good-bye as whoever is trying to reach you is growing impatient."

As if on cue, the unrelenting vibration repeated against his thigh, a reminder of Alana's irritation and impatience. "Okay, but this discussion is far from over. Let's get you home before Mr. Hyde breaks completely out of the cage I've been keeping him in and has his wicked way with you."

CHAPTER THIRTEEN

———

Daniel took a deep breath before slipping into the dark blue Cadillac. He made a mental note to have a word with his buddy about keeping his whereabouts private from the ladies, especially one as possessive as Alana. He didn't have proof a buddy had squealed, but it was the only way she could've known. No time like the present to face the music. "Hey, Alana, what's with blowing my phone up?"

The words had barely left his mouth when ruby red lips covered his and a small palm slid over his recently disappointed groin, quickly bringing it to life.

Grabbing her hand, and breaking the kiss, he held the long, manicured fingers where they couldn't cause damage. "You didn't answer my question."

The fiery redhead flashed him an angry glare. "You didn't tell me you were coming. I've been sitting at home, alone and missing you, while you were out doing god-knows-what with god-knows-who."

It wasn't quite that bad, but she knew him well enough to know if he was in town and not with her... "I'm sure your, what do they call them, sugar daddy, would be more than happy to spend time with you." Mr. Hyde returned with a vengeance—about time.

Tiny pin prickles of pain radiated from his cheek throughout his entire face. He could've stopped the slap but hoped she'd feel better afterward. It would help, making what came next easier.

"You know he pays little to no attention to me, and we haven't shared a bed in years. Not a secret I've kept from you."

A part of him felt bad for her. She wasn't married, but she enjoyed the finer things in life and a sugar daddy fit the bill. Unfortunately, she'd chosen a man who was many years older than her. She'd confessed he lost interest in sex years ago. Daniel couldn't help but wonder if the man physically couldn't perform or had simply lost interest. "It's a shitty problem, and it sucks for you, I know." The other part knew Alana wanted only one thing from him, and it had nothing to do with love.

Her hand slid between his legs as she moved closer. "A problem you've always been willing to help me with."

His manhood tightened uncomfortably under her experienced touch. She crooned, "C'mon, baby, we've had a lot of fun together. No strings—just like you want it."

She hit the nail right on the proverbial head. That was how he'd wanted it, but something was changing. He was changing. He didn't want to hurt Alana, but he couldn't do this anymore. He *had* wanted no strings attached before. Strings tied people down and restricted their freedoms. But, they also could hold people together. There was an hour and a half before he was supposed to meet Melodie. He needed to tell Alana good-bye and move on. It'd been a fun ride, but it was time to grow up and find the relationship his lonely heart deserved.

CHAPTER FOURTEEN

———

6:15. He was late. Melodie had chosen a seat at the oak bar adjacent to the lobby with a direct view of the front door. She'd checked with the front desk for messages. None. He didn't strike her as the type to not call. Though limited encounters, he'd been prompt to each meeting they'd set and respected the boundaries she'd given. The main problem? Even if she wanted to call him to make sure he hadn't been in an accident, they'd never exchanged cell phone numbers. He knew where she was staying, but otherwise, no way for them to communicate. She took another sip of her drink and thought back to their good-bye kiss this morning.

Never before had she been kissed so thoroughly—so intensely. Every fiber of her being begged her to invite him back to the room and fully experience everything this connection between them promised. She'd wanted to, but something held her back. Maybe the nagging at the back of her mind about the constant buzzing of his phone over the last several hours of their date? Maybe he'd decided she was toying with him, getting him all worked up, then not following through. Either way, he was a no-show. Disappointment settled low in her belly. Evelyn was right—she had no clue how to pick a man.

After draining the glass, she walked the short distance to the concierge desk to arrange a taxi. Adventure Melodie would go on. Though the past couple days had been a whirlwind, she liked the woman she was becoming or, perhaps, allowing herself to be the woman she'd always been. The plan was to see the JFK Memorial and see it she would—with or without him.

Her eyes widened at the sight before her. A magnificent memorial designed in tribute to Kennedy's brief, yet historical, life. The simple design consisted of four walls forming a monument to represent the freedom of Kennedy's spirit. The suspended structure lifted two feet above the ground on eight support beams that vanished the moment darkness fell and the lights around the memorial turned on, giving the structure the appearance of floating on light. Daniel had been right—mesmerizing.

She collapsed onto one of the benches outside the memorial and fought back an errant tear. This experience would mean so much more if someone were here to share in the moment. *Someone like Daniel.* A pity party loomed nearby, waiting to join and occupy her for as long as she'd allow the negative thoughts. Why couldn't she meet a nice guy and settle down? *Because I deserve more than nice, I deserve the storybook romance where Romeo sweeps me off my feet and kisses me until I forget how to spell my name.*

Dismissing Mr. Pity Party, she stared at the memorial, contemplating her life and wondering if it would end up as empty as the structure in front of her. As much as she cared for him, marrying Tom would've been a mistake. He deserved more too. They'd been comfortable with each other, the best of friends. Friends were all they would ever be though. His gentle touches didn't inflame her to heights of passion. Rather, they made her feel safe and cherished. At the time, she thought it would be all she ever wanted—all she deserved.

Tom was gone. Daniel, a no-show. Time to move on. No pity party today. Room service and a chick flick or disappearing inside the pages of a book sounded like a long overdue plan. She hailed a cab, ready to pick up the pieces and move forward yet again.

One chick-flick down and most of her steak devoured, Melodie sighed happily—nothing like a piece of perfectly cooked red meat to help ease heartache and disappointment. Throw in a baked potato and a piece of cheesecake for dessert and you'd guaranteed yourself at least an hour or so away from the harsh realities of life. They were still there. You just didn't care as much. The hotel phone ringing caused her to cough and spit out a piece of potato. Would Daniel be calling to apologize? Explain? With her heart pounding in her chest, she picked up the receiver.

"Hello."

"Melodie, it's your mother."

Her pounding heart immediately transformed into a pounding headache. "Oh, hi, Mom."

"Evelyn tells me you refuse to come home and meet this wonderful man she's found for you." Just like Mom. No pleasantries. Just right to the point. Less than one minute before Evelyn's name was brought up. How predictable their conversations had become. How Daddy had put up with her all these years was anyone's guess. He must be a candidate for sainthood or something.

"I'm doing great, Mom. Enjoying the vacation. Thanks for asking."

"Watch your tone, young lady, and answer my question."

"I don't need Evelyn to find a man for me, wonderful or not. I'm perfectly capable of doing that on my own." She wanted to believe that about herself anyway.

"Your track record suggests otherwise. Regardless, you're coming home for the party we're hosting later this week in Evelyn's honor."

It was a statement. A directive—not a question or a request.

Melodie refrained from a sarcastic comeback as that would only make the conversation longer and more painful. "What are we celebrating?"

"Evelyn settled a big case, earning millions in revenue for her firm." The maternal pride oozed through the phone and across half a country. "At this rate, they'll be putting her name first on the door."

"You must be very proud." She really was proud of her big sister, but her family never let her have the moment necessary to share. Evelyn had been shoved down her throat almost from birth, and though she resented the constant comparison, she knew her sister had worked hard and deserved every accolade she received. Melodie might need to have control over her own life, but Evelyn needed to control everyone and everything around her. Well, everyone except Mother.

"As you should be. Of course, if you only applied yourself half as much as Evelyn, you'd be earning more than the paltry paycheck you currently bring home. Honestly, Melodie, what kind of career is reading stories to children?"

Though she'd heard it time and time again, on the heels of Tom's death and the disillusionment with Daniel, the knife of her mother's disappointment drove deeper into her already fragile heart. A solitary tear slipped from her closely guarded control. "It's the kind of career that brings me joy and happiness, something that's never been a high priority for you."

"You will not speak to me with such disrespect, young lady."

"Good-bye, Mother." Melodie cut the connection before her mother's tireless rant could start again. She dialed the front desk. "Yes, please hold all my calls. No interruptions. Thank you."

She turned her cell on silent, dumped the remains of her dinner in the trash, grabbed the key, and headed out the door. Time to drown her sorrows at The Glass Cactus. Maybe Daniel's plan of love 'em and leave 'em wasn't so bad after all. The perfect plan actually. As long as you weren't the one being left.

CHAPTER FIFTEEN

─────

"What do you mean you can't ring her room? Is your switchboard broken?" Daniel's impatience with the incompetence of the staff at the hotel escalated with each passing moment.

"Sir, as I've explained for the last several minutes, Ms. Alexander has asked not to be interrupted. Would you like to leave a message?"

"No." Daniel paced the lobby of the grand hotel several times. Where in the hell was she? *I was late, very late...but she wouldn't answer the damn phone!* He hadn't meant to miss their date. Seeing the JFK Memorial with her at sunset would have ranked pretty damn high on the romance scale. Instead, he'd spent the last couple of hours breaking it off with Alana. He'd been tempted, so incredibly tempted, to take advantage of her willing body one last time, but the moment he closed his eyes, Melodie's silken brown hair and sweet smile replaced the predatory gleam of Alana's. His face still stung from her parting slap. See what happened when he tried to be a stand-up guy? Alana was no longer an option, and Melodie was nowhere to be found.

At least she hadn't checked out. If they're holding her calls, he still had a chance to make things right and explain. Of course, explaining why he'd been late would require courage. He'd never lacked courage before, but the *incident* had shaken his faith. In his country. In himself. Since Melodie was unavailable as a distraction, he decided to head to his favorite (translated closest) temporary distraction, The Glass Cactus.

He'd barely slugged down half a beer when he saw her. His wallflower—his beautiful wallflower, standing at the edge of the dance floor, glass of red liquid in hand, moving her hips subtly and sexily to the beat. Drawing in a calming breath, he made his way over to his jean-clad, peasant-bloused vixen. "You really should answer your phone."

The soft waves of her hair moved ever so slightly, shielding him from a direct glare. "You should learn to be on time."

The music blared, and the general cacophony of noise made the conversation he wanted to have with her impossible. "Can we step outside on the patio and talk?"

This time the hair tossed violently as she made an abrupt turn. Green eyes blazed with what he surmised to be anger before the light drained completely, leaving them dull and defeated. "I have nothing left to say. I'm obviously not your type. I'm moving on. You should do the same."

Melodie drained the contents of her glass before setting it on a nearby table. The heat of her body momentarily warmed him as she stepped past his form, making the resulting cold of her departure freeze his limbs with shards of distrust, disappointment, and disgust.

Just let her go.

He needed to let her go.

He wanted to let her go.

He couldn't let her go.

Tossing his half-empty bottle in the trash can, he wove through the growing crowd, never losing sight of his target. He had to explain—tell her why he'd been late. Last night he helped her with a makeup test by staying up all night, the least she could do was give him a second chance. Or was he on his third chance now? The moment they were both outside the doors, he vaulted into action. "Melodie, stop!"

* * *

At the sound of her name, she hesitated for only a second. The hesitation lasted one second too long. "What do you want, Daniel?" She kept her back to him, afraid if she looked into his eyes or drank in the male power he exuded so effortlessly, she'd get lost in a sea of emotions that would fill her lungs until she could no longer breathe.

His breath was hot on her neck and carried the faintest trace of ale. "I want to explain."

Her heart pleaded with her to listen, but her mind issued a strict warning. His presence was unsettling. She wanted safe…needed safe. "You don't owe me an explanation. You don't owe me anything. I'm not the kind of woman you usually pursue, I get that. I had a great time last night, and I thought you did too." She turned slowly, her gaze holding his. "If I had to guess, I'm thinking you were with whoever kept calling you this morning. Another woman? Or, God, do you have a girlfriend?" She felt sick. How could she have been so stupid?

His hand cupped her cheek as his lips christened her forehead. "Damn you, insufferable woman. I was late because I was telling the woman who kept calling that I didn't want to see her anymore." He lifted her face until her eyes focused solely on his. "After spending time with you, she pales in comparison."

Smooth talker. How can I believe him? He barely knows me. Her head shook as she disengaged his hand. "No, I've always been the runner up. I'm sure you'll see the error of your ways before the sun rises over the great state of Texas tomorrow."

All of the negative thoughts—about Daniel, her mother, and Evelyn retreated into darkness the moment his mouth crashed onto hers. His hands clutched at her blouse, holding her close and adding to the desperation of the kiss. He pulled her flush with his rock hard body, the contact spreading liquid fire through her veins, warming her everywhere they touched. Her knees threatened to buckle as he skillfully sent her emotions swirling, a vortex drawing her reluctantly—yet willingly— deeper and deeper into him. Immersed in a whirlwind of pleasure. Wanting to be needed. Needing to be wanted.

Breathless, she pulled back, trying to control the heaving of her chest expanding in direct opposition to the solid wall of his upper body. Damn, this man could kiss. "Why do you have to be so good at that?"

With a gentler kiss on the cheek, his whispered answer fanned across her ear. "I've found it the most effective way to get women to stop talking."

She wanted to argue, wanted to admonish him, wanted to kiss him again. "Well, it was nicer than a shut up, I suppose."

He chuckled. "Yeah, I've already been slapped a couple times tonight. Figured I'd take steps to avoid making my cheek even redder."

Hearing his confession, she gently caressed his cheeks with her hands. "Dare I ask what you did to get yourself slapped?"

"I told you. I broke up with door number two. She didn't take it so well."

The euphoria from the kiss slipped from her body almost as quickly as it surfaced. "I really wish you hadn't done that. I'm going home in a few days to Chicago. You're going home to…Good Lord, Daniel, I don't even know where you live."

"Mississippi."

She rolled her eyes at his statement. "Great. Long distance relationships rarely survive in romance books. We would have zero chance. Besides, my mother will confirm I'm nothing but a big disappointment anyway. You're just wasting your time."

"I have no idea what your mother has to do with any of this."

Melodie sighed. "You mean your mother isn't trying to control every facet of your life?"

"Not since I was sixteen. Before that we argued a lot." He grinned and kissed her forehead again.

"Well my mother has never outgrown that particular desire. She is bound and determined to find the perfect job, the perfect house, and, lest we forget, the perfect man for me. Or, at least, support Evelyn's choice for the job." Her voice sounded tired, even to her own ears.

He put his arm around her shoulders, gently guiding her back to the hotel. "I totally understand this is about more than you being pissed because I was late."

"Technically, you were a no-show. And, for the record, I am upset." Why she'd let this man get under her skin, she had no idea. *Because I want someone who can get under my skin and, maybe someday, into my heart.*

"Right. I was a no-show and I'm very sorry. I really wanted to see the memorial with you. I did try to reach you when I returned, but you weren't accepting calls. I'm guessing that was because your mom must've upset you earlier."

"You're pretty smart for a guy, aren't you?" For the first time all evening, a smile teased her lips. Nothing too overt. A hint of smile. More like a slight upturn of the corners of her mouth.

He stopped and cupped her cheek with his hand. "Not really, I just like paying attention to you." He combed his fingers through her hair before slipping his arm around her shoulders and resuming their walk.

She leaned in to him. "Score one more for Dr. Jekyll."

Once inside the sprawling interior of the hotel, she turned and smiled at him. "Enough talk about me. I'd rather talk about you and your breakup than discuss the sad state of my family affairs."

"Let me buy you a drink, and I'll give you the CliffsNotes. That's librarian talk, right? I remember my school librarian mentioning something about those."

Melodie rolled her eyes. He had a lot to learn about librarians. She added that to a list for another time and followed him the few steps to the lobby bar. Conflicted didn't even begin to describe the emotional storm barely held at bay deep within. His piercing blue eyes affected her on a frightening level. If she jumped into the deep end with him, would there be enough of her heart left should he turn out to be another in a long string of disappointments? Surprisingly, her heart won this battle. "One drink."

"What'll you two have?" The bartender offered a knowing smile aimed at Daniel.

"I'll take a beer, Coors light, and a vodka cranberry for the lady. Okay?" He took her hand and squeezed it.

She shook her head. She needed to keep her wits about her for important conversations with him. Daniel's effect on her had already reduced her normally logical brain to a mass of jumbled wires and nerves, making her engage in activities well outside the norm. "Diet soda, whatever you have."

Daniel smiled and glanced at the bartender. "You heard the lady. Two diet sodas and keep 'em coming."

His efforts to be a gentleman eased her worry—at least a fraction. Her heart continued gently tugging her toward the jumping off point for the deep end.

"Thank you." At Daniel's smile, she shrugged her shoulders. "I need the caffeine. Plus, I want to be sure I don't miss one word of whatever you have to say to me. It's been a crappy day that I'd love nothing more than to improve, so, I'm listening."

Daniel leaned in and kissed her on the cheek. "Sure as hell has been, especially for one that started off on such a good note."

"Feels like a lifetime ago now." She sipped a fair amount of the carbonated caffeine, relishing the way it released hidden energy. Hard to believe a little over twelve hours had elapsed since the best night of her life. Ironic how quickly life could take a nosedive complete with a one-hundred-eighty-degree twist. She wanted to focus on the good and returned her full attention to the present.

Daniel took a long draw of his soda. She couldn't help but notice his sensual lips. A darker shade of pink but not quite red. They were full, soft, and capable of rendering her unable to string two words together in a logical pattern. She refused to give consideration to what they might feel like skimming over the rest of her body, venturing to places rarely visited by a man's hands or lips. *Focus.*

"So, tell me what happened."

One more swig. Whether it was to delay answering or some other reason, Melodie wasn't sure. She prayed whatever he said wouldn't prove an end to what had been a tumultuous, but potentially major life-turning, couple of days.

"Remember my philosophy about women?"

How could I forget? She nodded. "Cause and effect which brought you to a love 'em and leave 'em or, as I like to call it, use 'em and lose 'em kind of deal."

His face darkened. "Sounds worse when you put it like that."

Another drink and she shrugged. "I call it like I see it."

Daniel's long fingers combed through the military cut of his dark blond hair, "You've got the story wrong for this woman. She used me like I used her. It was mutual. We both took what we needed. No strings. No expectations."

A relationship of convenience. A small pang of guilt put her on edge. She and Tom had found each other convenient as well. "I understand why you preferred the arrangement. Why did she?"

"She's not leaving her sugar daddy. He has little to no interest in a physical relationship with her from what she's shared with me."

"Doesn't that make her the perfect woman for you?" The sarcasm rolled from her tongue, sadly with practiced ease. He was sharing a part of himself, and that scared her.

He drained the soda and signaled for another round to the bartender. Deep sapphire hues drilled into her heart, letting her see all the way into his soul, bared and exposed, as the next words slipped out of his elegant mouth. "It did. Right until the moment I met you."

Her entire body felt heavy. Had he just confessed to leaving his previously ideal woman because of her? Even after she'd refused his advances—well, most of them anyway—and wouldn't invite him to her hotel room? "What are you saying?" It wasn't eloquent, but the best she could muster at the moment—at least she didn't stutter.

He moved his bar stool closer to hers until his inner thighs rested on either side of her now trembling legs. She swallowed hard, trying to ignore the heat radiating from his body drawing her into his sensual web. Helpless and awaiting her fate.

"I'm saying I enjoy your company, and when I'm with you, I find myself wanting to change old habits. I'm not a perfect guy, but you already know that."

The corners of her mouth turned up a little at his admission. "Jekyll and Hyde as I recall."

"But much sexier than either of those two."

Deep end, here I come. Her hands developed a mind and will of their own as they moved to rest on his knees for a few moments before sliding up his muscular thighs. She was certain they quivered under her touch. "Much sexier."

Larger hands covered hers. "I want to tell you everything, even though you didn't ask. It's my way of earning your trust. As you guessed, she was the one calling me this morning. A buddy of mine must've let it slip I was in town, and she's very possessive. Didn't like that I hadn't called or stopped by yet. I went to break it off with her. She wasn't happy but agreed to let me go. She just wanted to…"

The ice-cold water of reality poured over Melodie faster than Gatorade over a winning coach's head. She abruptly pulled her hands back. *Moving away from the ledge by the deep end now…*"God, can't you go without it for twenty-four hours? I turned you down so you thought, why not? One last roll in the hay with your bed buddy?" She'd heard it referred to as something cruder, but years of working with children kept her from saying the F word out loud, even if she occasionally thought it.

He grabbed her hands, pulling her upper body close to him again, leaving her balancing precariously on the tall stool. Much harder to ignore his male presence and power this close. No wonder the other woman wanted one last go with him. Her heart begged her to keep backing away from the ledge.

"She wanted me to, but I shut her down. Which, by the way, earned me another slap. Extricating myself from her claws and her car took longer than I thought. That's why I was late."

He released her abruptly, causing her to teeter a bit on the stool. Traitorous hands sought purchase on his rock hard thighs, stabilizing her. The impact of his words wound around her like the silken thread of the spider, holding her captive. Was it really worth the struggle to try to escape? Could this spider have changed his markings? From the beginning, he'd told her that whatever this was, he wanted to explore. Now he'd put action to the words. Could she do the same and change a lifetime of keeping people at an arm's distance to protect her heart?

Doing relationships her way always landed her squarely in the loser's column in the game of love. Hollow and wounded on the inside, never truly letting anyone in. Tom had gotten closer than anyone, and she'd never forget the way he loved her, even though their affection spoke more of a deep friendship and convenience, rather than passionate love. Still, she'd loved him in her own way. He'd always hold a very special place in the part of her heart she kept hidden away from others. But perhaps now—now was the time for exploring uncharted territory and venturing outside the pages of her books, outside her comfort zone.

Leaning in closer, she kissed the pulse point on his neck, inhaling the spicy scent, creating a memory moment. *Here we go.* Time to jump into the deep end. "Daniel, will you join me in my room?"

CHAPTER SIXTEEN

———

This woman's quickly changing moods put him at risk for whiplash. The current shift, however, included a never-before-offered invitation to her hotel room. After turning him down for two days, he had no idea what brought about the change, but his momma didn't raise no fool. No way was he going to miss an opportunity to spend time in this beautiful—albeit complex—woman's bed. *Don't blow this. She's special. I want more than one night.*

Cupping her cheek, he pulled her even closer, sliding his lips across hers. The faint taste of her lip gloss lent itself to a much sweeter mingling than the beer taste of his usual companions. Her lips parted slightly under his, and a soft *mmmm* escaped. The verbalized sound of pleasure went straight to his groin and made it very difficult to remain the gentleman. Pulling away slightly, he couldn't resist the urge to slip his thumb across her satiny lips. "I love kissing you and am looking forward to even more. First, though, I need you to tell me what happened earlier today in your neck of the woods."

Her face registered a slight pinch of disappointment.

Yeah, being shut down sucks, doesn't it?

She finished off her drink before sighing heavily. "Do you really want to talk about my mother right now?"

Hell no! "Turnabout's fair play and all. I've talked about my ex and my recently departed—what did you call her? Bed buddy?"

"Smart-ass."

There was the smile he loved. Between her smile and those eyes, he'd never look at another woman the same way. "Better than being called a dumb one, I've heard."

She graced him with a small bit of laughter before her expression quickly sobered. "I suppose so."

A slight twinge of guilt pricked at him for pushing her. He didn't regret the decision to delay the trip to her room though. He wanted to have all their cards on the table before he made her forget about every love scene she'd ever read. *Well, not all my cards. Enough for one day. The explosion and everything that happened after. Not going there. Not now. She doesn't need that kind of complication.*

"There's not much to tell, really. Same old story. Evelyn is a grand success. Let's celebrate Evelyn and all she's accomplished. Why can't I be more like Evelyn?" Her waves of brown hair shook in disgust. "It sounds trite and overused, even to me. I'm sorry."

An overwhelming sense of urgency settled deep in his heart, fueling an overriding need to protect this woman from her family and, maybe, even from herself. From what he'd learned, she'd spent a lifetime in her sister's shadow and her mother's unrelenting comparisons.

Was that how his brothers and sisters felt?

He pulled her into a hug. "Hey, come on now. You're intelligent, caring, beautiful, and compassionate. Truthfully, one of the most incredible women I've met. We each follow the orders of our own drill sergeants. Trust me when I say, keeping your assigned drill instructor happy is all that matters. It's her loss if she can't see you for the amazing woman you are."

He disengaged from the embrace and held her face between his hands. "Let me show you."

Her slight nod provided the only confirmation he needed. Paying the bartender, he joined their hands and let her lead the way to her room. For the first time in his life, something more than physical gratification topped the agenda. He wanted— no, needed—to show Melodie how special she truly was. She made him want to change. Made him see the need to change. Made him believe in the possibility of love again.

The release of the electronic lock reverberated loudly in the quiet resting between them. The door opened to a spacious room. The standard cream and browns colored the room along with dark furniture. The king-size bed dominated the area, and he couldn't help but smile. He pictured Melodie snuggled under the covers, her body taking up very little space. Oh yes, she definitely needed his body mass taking up some room and getting the most use out of this vast piece of real estate. Against the back wall, sliding glass doors provided entry to the balcony. The wall mirror, though, caught his eye, providing a clear path to his next step in this adventure. The moment the door shut, he pulled her into a tight hug. Her soft curves pressing into his body tested his resolve. He'd wanted this woman almost from the beginning, and now here they were. The proverbial gates of heaven were within his reach. All he needed to do was take those few steps forward. *Do. Not. Screw. This. Up.* "Are you sure?"

She nodded against his chest. "I'm not sure what this is, but whatever it is, I want to explore it."

Kissing the top of her head, he moved them until they were standing in front of the mirror, her back to his front. "I want you to keep your eyes open so I can show you what I see—what others see when they look at you. Forget about your mother, your sister…everyone else who lacks the brains to recognize the true value of the woman standing right in front of them."

With a slowness that belied the impatience coursing through his body, he slid his fingers through her hair, tousling it into sexy disarray. "I noticed your hair first. Waves of chocolate with a hint of fire. From the moment you dipped your head on the plane to avoid my gaze, I've wanted to do this. So soft—so beautiful."

His hands circled her neck, fingers lifting her chin slightly. "Your eyes—those amazing emerald eyes. I wish I read books and studied like you so I could find the right words to tell you how brilliant and breathtaking they are. They've kept me coming back for more, despite your immunity to all my best moves and lines. Any other woman, I would have made my retreat and sought out friendlier territory."

He stared at her face in the mirror until she made eye contact. Emerald jewels sparkling in the faint light. She'd captured a small piece of her bottom lip between her teeth. *Sexy vulnerability.* Not wanting her to doubt for one second the power of her appeal, he offered a small reassuring smile as he caressed a couple fingers over her mouth, down her cheek, and along the smooth line of her neck.

Letting his hands slide lower, fingers deftly worked the buttons of her blouse, one by one. Her soft breasts rose and fell as her breathing deepened. Drawing in a few long breaths, he fought to steady his trembling hands. Every ounce of blood necessary for rational thought raced below the waistband of his jeans as creamy flesh framed in black lace came into view. He busied himself with kisses in the curve of her neck to keep from saying something that would fall under the "total guy" column. Once her blouse floated to the floor, his right hand went over her heart. Hands and lips experienced the wild racing of her pulse as he whispered against her skin. "I love how your heart beats so strong and passionate. Can you feel it? Can you feel your blood heating with desire?"

Throaty. Husky. Breathy. "Yes. God, yes."

"Good. This same heart is generous, kind, and compassionate. No one becomes a children's librarian who doesn't have a great capacity to love and give. Children sense that. My daughter can spot a fake a mile away. So can her dad. You're the real thing." His heart finally connected with his brain as he realized all the other women had merely been substitutions. Warmth filled his chest and spurred him on.

"Daniel, I...standing...very hard. Please..."

Deep, calming breaths helped him stay on task. Getting close now. "Patience." Even as the words left his mouth, his arousal pressed hard against the confines of his jeans. Her breasts fit perfectly into his hands. Slow circles around the tips provided the desired response. "Beautiful, responsive, and sexy."

The only answer he received came in an arching back, her body demanding more of his touch. He could do that. With a quick pinch of the pebbled tips, eliciting a gasp from those sensuous lips, he skimmed down her torso and made quick work of the fastenings holding the denim jeans in place, lowering them until the length of her firm thighs and legs were all he could see. He drank in the revealed skin through her reflection. "Open your eyes. See what I see."

Green eyes met blue in the mirror. "And what do you see?"

"I've run out of adjectives. Hell, I'd be repeating myself. So let me say something to you that will mean more than this jarhead could ever come up with on his own."

Stepping out of her jeans, she turned in his embrace, her face only inches from his—her arms holding him close. "What words would you say?"

This was it, his moment of truth. A moment he'd been waiting a lifetime to happen. "I'd say I see someone I want to spend more than one night with."

* * *

Her free fall into the deep end continued. Did her self-proclaimed bad boy confess he wanted more from her than a one-night stand? Though she'd only known him a few days, her hands-on research on this subject revealed this admission to be a huge leap from the normal way he operated. He wanted her and...he wanted her for more than tonight. He'd made her feel like the most desirable woman in the world. Her whispered response could barely be heard over the wild pounding of her heart. "Take me to bed."

Any remaining thoughts of family drama slithered back into a dark corner of her mind when Daniel's lips crushed down on her waiting mouth as his body tightened against hers. The hard planes of his chest cut into her softness.

Tracing her fingers over his stubbled jaw spiked her desire to feel more of his skin. Heat radiated from his body, the warmth infusing every pore, every facet of her existence in this moment. She slid her hands lower, travelling down his back until the hem of his T-shirt rested between her fingers. She tugged upward, the need to feel his skin against her driving her into action. The smallest of spaces emerged between their bodies— just enough for material to slide between them. Tearing her mouth away from his to catch a quick breath and remove the shirt, she slowed the frenzy in her brain long enough to focus on his silky skin. Her turn to explore. Wanting to return some of the pleasure he'd been so patiently giving her, she smoothed her hands over his chest. The hitch in his breath drawing her into the deep end...drowning in everything that was and is Daniel. She wanted more...needed more. She eased him backward until his knees hit the bed. Amost there. She smoothed her hands over the taut muscles of his chest up to his shoulders. A gentle push guided him lower and lower until he reclined fully on the bed.

His deeply tanned body against the light colored bedspread spurred visions of chocolate and cream—two of her favorite things.

Greek Adonis more than knight in shining armor.

Not wanting to delay this any further or before she could chicken out, her fingers fumbled with the button of his Levi's.

Dear God...he has THOSE muscles.

She traced a finger along his pelvic bone, the well-defined muscle outlining the area leading her lower to the promise of satisfaction. The blood he so expertly heated minutes ago rushed to the center of her core, throbbing with intensity, rendering it impossible for her legs to hold her vertical any longer.

"Come here. Don't leave me on this big bed alone."

Her attention shifted to the whole of his magnificent body. Slow, seductive sensations spread throughout every limb as he shrugged out of his jeans.

Oh yeah, guess I should've finished that.

He retrieved a square foil package from his wallet and then tossed the clothing and the wallet on the floor.

"Always prepared, I see." The gaping need to feel his body over her, in her, around her defied the cautious logical woman she'd always been.

"Always." He pulled her until she tumbled next to him on the bed. Moments later, she got the first wish—his body over hers.

Hot breath against her skin created shivers of desire. Daniel slid a finger under one of the straps on her bra, moving it away from her shoulder, before anointing the area with tender kisses. She murmured a sigh of pleasure when his tongue swept across the swell of her breast. Need pulsed through her veins stronger than anything she'd ever felt before. *So good.* She writhed under his skilled touch, wanting more...so much more. .

"Mmm....oh yes...there..." followed by gasps and other incoherent sounds, apparently the only words she could string together as he moved slowly down her body, lavishing unparalleled attention on every inch.

"I want to be better." Daniel whispered as he reached behind her and unclasped her bra, removing the garment to join the others on the floor.

His words made her blink rapidly, trying to focus. "Better? Better than whom?"

His mouth closed around a pebbled tip, making her gasp. *He is better. Better than anyone...* "This is better..."

His teeth grazed the tips, sending shards of pleasure slicing through her body.

"So. Much. Better." She could barely speak, her words more of a husky whisper.

Daniel's inactivity left her no choice but to force her eyes, weighted heavy with need, open. The crystal blue color of his eyes, now dark and intense, was trained completely on her. "I want to be better—want us to be better—than all the love scenes you've read in those books."

He might possibly be the sweetest man she'd ever met. She cupped his cheek with her hand. "Don't go too sweet on me. I like a little spice, remember? The books are great, but you..." Her hand slid down to his granite chest, her nails lightly scraping the golden skin. "You are the real thing."

Maybe the most "real" man she'd ever met. No hiding who he was or, more importantly, his motives. She didn't want to think anymore—only feel. She wrapped her legs around his hips and pulled his lower body closer. His impressive arousal twitched impatiently between their bodies, deepening and intensifying the ache between her legs. If she didn't get relief soon...

Raking long nails across his back rewarded her with a low moan and a nip at the swell of her breast. "And all those love scenes pale in comparison to you."

"You ain't seen nothin' yet, darlin'." This time, she didn't mind the arrogance. So far, he'd earned every right to brag on his bedroom prowess.

The words from countless love scenes she'd read flashed across her mind before vanishing under Daniel's expert touch. His mouth blazed a path of fire lower and lower.

He's trying to kill me.

No wonder he only needs one night. The women never live to experience a second night. "Daniel, please…"

Daniel's body slid up hers until their mouths clashed. His tongue demanded entrance, cutting off any further verbal comment. She held his body as close as possible, her legs locking behind his hips, rocking against silken steel, inviting him to finish what he'd started.

He tore away from the kiss, his breath shallow and fast. "Ready?"

She arched her body and rocked against him again, "For what feels like hours now."

The arrogant grin covered his face—she didn't even care. He'd earned it. "I've been ready for days, woman."

CHAPTER SEVENTEEN

———

She held him close, the welcome weight of a lover resting fully in her arms once again. His body was nothing short of perfect. Sculpted, tanned, and currently all hers. A Greek Adonis inviting her to this sweet escape.

"That was incredible." She danced her fingertips along the smooth line of his back, continuing the intimacy of the moment. Maybe one night would be acceptable, as long as the night never ended. She wanted to somehow thank him for such a wonderful gift. For his promise of wanting more than a one-night stand, even if she wasn't sure either could follow through. Distance proved a powerful force in any relationship. Maybe they could connect every few months for a weekend or something until they knew whether their hearts could allow them both the happiness they deserved.

Evelyn taunted her from the time-out corner she'd put her in after their last conversation, reminding her of why she'd chosen Tom. *"...you only chose him because he was away most of the time."* Was that true? Did she only want a relationship with a man who wouldn't be around all the time? Damn Evelyn for finding her way into even the most private of her moments.

"You're welcome, and you're right. It was incredible. Just as I'd imagined." Soft kisses roused her from her thoughts. "You okay?"

Melodie held him tight, trying not to think about how perfectly their bodies fit together. She kissed him gently. "Better than okay. Thank you again for…well, for everything."

The cocky grin returned. "I'd say the pleasure was all mine, but…"

The Hallmark moment ruined, she pushed him off her body, smiling as she made her way to the bathroom. "But I had a little too."

"Little? Woman, were you paying attention at all?" A very unladylike and unusual squeal slipped out of her mouth as Daniel tackled her from behind, picking her up and twirling her around.

Feeling sexy, desirable and, yes, maybe a little like the heroine in a romance novel who had just secured the bad boy, she wiggled her hips against him. "Apparently not enough. Maybe you'll have to demonstrate for me again."

Rough, work-hewn hands cupped her breasts as he held her close, arousing and warming her all over again. "I'm sure that can be arranged. Since someone kept me up last all night, maybe a little sleep is in order first?"

She turned in his embrace, trying to keep the surprise off her face. "Are you asking to spend the night?"

The cocky expression morphed for only a second into a look of vulnerability before a composed, neutral expression settled over his cheekbones and stubbled chin. "If you're not comfortable with that..."

She shook her head. "No. I mean yes. Wait..." she took a deep breath. "What I'm trying to say is I'd like you to stay." *His ability to render me speechless continues. Gotta work on that.*

"Can I order a pizza? I'm starving."

The grin returned, and she was certain there was a hint of relief in his tone. "Veggie?"

"Ugh, you've got to be kidding? Half veggie, half meat lovers?"

Standing on her tiptoes, she kissed his cheek. "Deal. You make the call. I'm gonna grab a shower."

"I'll make the call and then join you in the shower."

Humming a few bars of "Sweet Dreams," she turned on the water—hot. Her body would be sore from the paces Daniel put her through and, she held hope deep in her tattered heart, there would be plenty more activity still to come. The hot water beaded on her skin, reminding her of Daniel's ardent touch. The cool whoosh of air created goose bumps all over her body, but they disappeared the moment Daniel's body surrounded hers. She closed her eyes. Maybe all of this was too good to be true. Or maybe this time she'd finally find her little slice of happiness.

CHAPTER EIGHTEEN

———

Daniel roused from sleep. Melodie was standing at the sliding glass doors, staring off into space. Silently, he applauded her ability to even stand. After pizza and another vigorous round of lovemaking, he didn't even have the energy to move. He couldn't stop smiling as he thought about how magnificent Melodie looked above him, her breasts swaying freely as she rode him—hard. He refused to think too far ahead, but he damn well liked this woman more than anyone else he'd met in a very long time—if ever.

With her standing there in nothing but his T-shirt and pink, silk boy shorts, Daniel's need for her resurfaced. *I may never get enough of this woman.*

Not wanting to waste one moment of their time together, he crept quietly out of bed and moved in behind her, his arms circling her waist. "Hey, sexy, you up for another round?"

As he kissed her cheek, instead of the fresh clean scent he'd become accustomed to, there was a hint of salt and dampness. Tears? What the hell? "What's wrong?"

Her hands pulled him closer as she sank into his embrace. "There's something I haven't told you."

Just when he thought it was safe… "Come on. Let's go back to bed. We'll talk. You can tell me anything." Her soft bottom pressed against his groin made talking the last thing he wanted to do, but a man's gotta do what a man's gotta do.

He followed her back to bed and tried not to focus on her bare legs sliding under the sheet. *Behave!* He didn't want her to kick him out and send him skulking back to his room in the wee hours of the morning. He tried not to think of the number of times he'd sent a woman packing from his room in the middle of the night. Turning the light on the nightstand to the lowest level, he slipped in next to her, pulling her close. His arm went around her shoulders to offer comfort. "Tell me, Mel. Whatever it is, it can't be that bad."

"His name was Tom."

She made her statement as if those four words would allow him to decipher and fix whatever was upsetting her. He'd known lots of Toms in his life, none of which he could remember making him cry. He had no clue what to say. "Go on. I'm listening."

"He was my best friend. We understood each other. He always thought Evelyn was too good to be true and stood up for me against my mother. He was a good man." She smiled faintly. "We'd even made a pact to marry at age thirty if we were both still single."

He might not be a librarian or college graduate, but even he recognized the past tense. He ignored the little detail about her marriage plans. "You keep saying was. What happened to him?"

"He made me feel safe, secure, and content. Evelyn says I only chose him because he was away most of the time. Maybe she was right. I don't know. I do know he didn't deserve what happened to him."

The haunted look he'd seen in her eyes numerous times since their first chance meeting on the plane returned. This man, Tom, whatever happened to him, must be responsible for the sadness in her eyes. His protective instincts surged, and he felt compelled, driven even, to make this better. *Once she tells me what in the hell happened to him.* Did women always take this long to share? Up to this point, he'd only cared about pretending to listen long enough to get into their bed. The clouded green eyes from his sexy librarian changed all of that for him.

"What happened to him?" He felt like a broken record, but maybe if he kept asking, eventually she'd tell him.

"He was killed."

His muscles tightened, and his nostrils flared. He'd seen so much death in Afghanistan—so much senseless death. A war being waged by politicians saddled with the high cost of human life. To think this man had been murdered on American soil, outside of war, fueled his rage at the injustice. "Did they catch the bastard?"

The confusion in her eyes deepened. "What?"

"The person who murdered him."

Tears escaped down her cheeks again before she buried her face in his shoulder. Why did women do that? Didn't they know it rendered the male species unable to think clearly? A few drops of water sliding down rosy cheeks reduced every goal in their lives down to one. Fix whatever's wrong, and make it better so she stops crying.

"He wasn't murdered. He was killed in action in Afghanistan."

Afghanistan brought his mind into sharp focus. He may have not known her Tom, but he knew plenty of men like him. He fought to stop the trembling of his body. *Breathe, dammit.* Had someone snuck into his little slice of heaven and punched him in the gut? He fought the strong desire to jump out of the warmth of the bed and pace. His questions now expelled in rapid fire. "What happened to Tom? How was he killed?"

If his harsh tone insulted Melodie, she offered no comment. "His convoy was on an errand of mercy, delivering food and supplies to a village hit hard in an attack. The lead vehicle, Tom's vehicle, hit one of those bombs buried in the road...an IBD or something?"

The blows to his gut continued with each innocent word she spoke. Guilt squeezed his heart so tightly radiating pain shot down his left arm. *Heart attack?* "IED. Improvised explosive device."

"Yes, that's it. Sorry. I couldn't bring myself to do any research on the subject, too upsetting."

He wanted to say something to comfort her, reassure her. Something! But the words wouldn't come. His throat filled with sand, scratching every surface. He squeezed her tighter in reassurance, hoping to God it would be enough.

Her body moved in closer as she slipped farther under the covers. The tension she'd been holding slowly left her limbs, allowing her body to relax. "My heart hurts less now that you're in my life. I know it sounds crazy, but somehow you've eased the pain."

His eyes closed when her face lifted to kiss him. He couldn't open them—couldn't let her see the torment. Couldn't take a chance the guilt in his eyes would prompt the return of the haunted look he'd noticed the first time they met. Instead, he focused on her soft, sweet lips against his. He squeezed his eyes even tighter, concentrating on exactly how she felt in his arms

As her body relaxed against his, the tightness in his chest limited his ability to breathe. Not only had he seen death in Afghanistan, but he'd had a front row seat to the mayhem. Wanting to block the painful memories, he forced the air slowly in and out of his lungs. Her delicate scent calmed the racing of his heart, allowing him to compartmentalize the negative emotions threatening to consume him. In and out. Focus on each breath. It wasn't his fault.

Too bad he couldn't make himself believe that, no matter how hard he tried.

CHAPTER NINETEEN

———

Tuesday

Bacon. The hickory smoke flavor filled the air along with the blissful aroma of coffee. Her stomach rumbled, demanding attention. "Daniel?"

"Room service just arrived. Hungry?"

She sat up. The white-covered table boasted a crystal vase with a single red rose. *Straight out of a romance novel.* Even better than the rose were two plates heaping with the ultimate representation of a Southern hospitality breakfast. Her meal included bacon, eggs, hash browns, biscuits, even grits and gravy. She'd never had grits and gravy, but there'd been lots of things she'd tried in the last day or so that were new. So far, so good. "I'm starving. Someone worked up quite an appetite in me last night."

Grabbing his T-shirt—his chest looked even better uncovered—she slipped it on and moved to the table. "No breakfast in bed I guess?" She smiled at the hurt look on his handsome face. "I'm teasing, relax."

His fingers combing through her hair delivered shivers of delight careening down her spine, almost making her forget how hungry she was. Almost.

"If you'd like to crawl back into bed, I'll be happy to serve you. Something tells me we'd skip right to dessert."

As a distraction, she plucked a warm piece of bacon from the plate and bit off a decent amount. "Mmm. As delicious as dessert sounds, I need to eat something to keep my strength up. Sit. Eat."

Soft, coffee-tasting lips covered hers momentarily, ceasing the enjoyment of her bacon. The gentleness of the kiss was distinctly different from the passion they'd shared in the early hours of the morning. She couldn't put her finger on the difference exactly, which reminded her of the pending "how to read people" research. His fingers trailed softly along her cheek and down her throat. Warmth. Gentleness.

"Yes ma'am. Let's eat."

The food tasted better than anything she'd eaten since arriving in the great state of Texas. Maybe her stomach was adjusting to the southwest spices infused in every meal. *Maybe my heart is starting to heal.* After another sip of coffee, she consumed enough food and caffeine to carry on meaningful conversation. "Thank you again for your understanding in the wee hours of the morning. I've been working through my grief and thought I had it under control." She paused, unsure of how much she could say without revealing how hard she'd fallen for him. "Anyway, thanks for listening. What are your plans for today?"

He shrugged and pushed the food on his plate around some more. "Not a problem. As to my plans, I'm not sure."

"What's wrong? You've barely eaten anything."

His face lifted, blue eyes entering her line of vision. Her stomach clenched as recognition dawned. The ice blue eyes displayed the familiar haunted look she'd caught in her own reflection at times. The bacon and biscuits started flip-flopping in her stomach. Did he regret being with her? Had her middle-of-the-night confession changed his mind about her? "Daniel? Please tell me what's wrong."

The table jarred at his abrupt rise from the chair. "I don't want to."

In direct opposition to his movement, her slow rise allowed her hands to grip the edge tightly, a concerted effort to control the trembling—from fear? "I shared intimate details from my heart last night. You can tell me anything. I know about your ex and your mistress—your womanizing ways. Can't be much else to shock me, right?" The pitch of her voice rose with each phrase, amplifying the fear that last night was too good to be true.

"Men, probably a lot like your Tom, died in Afghanistan. Died because of me."

The free fall into the deep end finished with her heart hitting the concrete at the bottom hard, crushing her chest and making it difficult to breathe. The violent shaking of her head confirmed her adamant denial. "What do you mean? You and Tom were on the same side. How could you possibly be responsible for the death of an American soldier?" She'd heard the term friendly fire before but couldn't imagine Daniel, even at his worst, making a mistake and shooting the wrong person.

"After I retired from the military, I worked for a while as a civilian contractor. Because of my familiarity with the terrain, my job included leading both military and civilian personnel through any number of missions. Humanitarian convoys, like you mentioned with Tom, or strategic ops to gain intel. Really, anything my employer ordered. Once a soldier, always a soldier."

With each word, the beating of her heart gained momentum. She forced thoughts of Tom to the back of her mind. It was evident Daniel was suffering. He'd helped her through the pain last night. She would do the same for him. "Tell me what happened. I may not be able to fully understand, but sometimes talking things out is good for you. Telling you about what happened to Tom last night proved very therapeutic for me. Let me do the same for you."

Strong hands—hands that had brought her so much pleasure over the past several hours—held her arms in a vice-like grip. "No. No one, especially a woman, wants to hear about my mistakes and failures. Hell, I'm tired of thinking about them myself." He released her and sunk onto the bed, his hands holding his head. "All you need to know is you deserve better, so much better. For a moment I allowed myself to believe… But I was wrong." Unshed tears glinted in the troubled depths.

Way out of my depth, but I have to try. "I don't believe that for a minute, but if you feel that way, tell me why. Help me understand."

He patted the space on the bed next to him, but her feet refused to move. Instead, she knelt down in front of him and rested her hands on his knees. His eyes closed for a moment while his chest contracted and expanded, breath struggling to enter and leave his lungs. She refused to focus on how well the muscles framing his chest and abs felt pressed against her body. How safe she'd been in his arms.

When he opened his eyes and stared directly at her gaze, she saw it. The guilt, the pain, the regret—she could almost see the heavy weight of emotion pulling him down. He'd been able to keep this hidden from her, only glimpses of the pain coming through. But now, after all they had shared, maybe he would let her completely in—see who he really was. His head moved slowly and it took her a moment to realize he was shaking it. "I don't want to talk about this. I want to forget it and move forward."

Her hands squeezed his thigh tighter, trying to offer reassurance. "Daniel, you obviously can't move forward. I know *we* can't move forward until you deal with this." She leaned in closer and kissed him on the cheek. "I really like you and want to explore…how did you phrase it? Whatever this is. I'm a good listener. Let's work through this together."

The faraway look on his face intensified the pain in her heart. "This was another in a long line of mistakes I've made. I'm sorry." The finality in his voice saddened her. He was giving up. On himself and, by shutting her out, on further exploration between the two of them.

All of the negative emotions settled in the center of her heart. "I was nothing more than a mistake to you? I don't really believe you mean it, but if that's how you want to play this, I don't know what more to say." She kissed him on the cheek again and searched his face for any sign of a change of heart. Nothing. Not even a glance from those gorgeous blue eyes. Nothing but the downward tilt of those beautiful lips—lips that had made her smile and brought so much pleasure. The transformation was heartbreaking. She sighed and started to pack her things, time to go home.

CHAPTER TWENTY

————

Melodie stumbled into her drab, one bedroom apartment, praying the comfort of home would ease the heart-wrenching pain tormenting her from the moment she stepped outside of her hotel room. She'd left Daniel, hurting and hiding behind his pain. She'd wanted him to explain, practically begged him to share with her. He'd made love to her, made her feel like the most amazing woman in the world and shut her out precisely at the moment she'd been willing to step outside the pages of the books she'd been hiding behind.

She flung herself onto the couch, tears falling unhindered. Every muscle, every inch of her body hurt. The strain from the emotional roller coaster she'd been on for months now begged for release. She cursed the war, cursed Tom for leaving her to serve, and cursed Daniel for showing her a side of herself she didn't realize existed. Damn them all!

Exhaustion won the battle over emotion, and she succumbed to sleep once the supply of tears dried up. The cycle started over as her eyes slowly opened. This time, however, the focus had changed. Images of Daniel flashed through her mind and left her with one resounding stream of thought. Daniel needed her as much as she needed him. The war hurt them both, in similar yet different ways.

Hot tears, a fresh supply from somewhere, burned her cheeks as realization slammed into her. His pain, the cocky arrogance, the haunted look in his eyes, each and every one a signal his wounds ran as deep as hers—mostly likely even deeper. The war may not have taken his life, but it robbed him of the belief he deserved happiness. And what had she done? Let a lifetime of messed-up relationships make her leave before she could force him to explain, to talk things through, to kiss and makeup.

She hugged the pillow tighter, grief consuming her to the depths of her soul. Minutes morphed into hours until the waterworks, as her mother termed them, dried up. Thankfully, no one knew she'd come home early, so they'd leave her alone until she could pull herself together enough to face them, their criticism, and their instruction on how to "fix" her life.

Work. Work would help her find the balance in her life again. The children. The books. *The escape.* Daniel's presence challenged everything she thought she knew about herself, her choices, and her wants. *I want him.* She pulled her sorry butt off the bed and lumbered into the bathroom. Some cold water on her face and a hot shower for her body—just what the doctor ordered. *Dr. Jekyll and Mr. Hyde.*

The cold water from the sink spelled relief to her red, puffy eyes. Hopefully, the swelling and discoloration would disappear. Otherwise, the children would be frightened. They'd probably tell her she looked like a character from *The Spooky Series* she read to them each Halloween. A glimpse of red with a white, weird shaped "X" on it caught her eye—Daniel's shirt. She'd been wearing it as they ate breakfast this morning—before everything went horribly wrong.

Inhaling deeply, she smelled his cologne. A spicy, manly scent, but the name escaped her. There were too many memories from their all-night adventure to remember such a detail. *More research to add to the list.* She removed it carefully before running a hot bath. The shirt and the faint scent were all that remained of the man who'd snuck in and stolen her heart right from underneath her nose.

Slipping under the bubbles, her eyes closed. Images of Daniel's smile, the cocky way he held his head, and the intensity in those cerulean depths as he peered into her very soul flooded her mind, making relaxation impossible. She drew a deep breath. Enough of the pity party. She'd learned enough about herself over the past few days to know she'd changed…for the good. The corners of her mouth turned upward in a small smile. Though she had no reason to believe it, no way to reach him, nothing but a T-shirt to hold onto, something inside her romance-novel-loving heart told her their story wasn't quite finished.

CHAPTER TWENTY-ONE

―――――

Thursday

Thank God his dream girl's occupation was a children's librarian and not an employee of the secret service. Finding her required some time but posed little difficulty. The last few days had been pure hell as he fought his greatest enemy—himself.

When she left, hurt and upset at his refusal to talk about *that* day, his first inclination had been to hit the bar. He'd let the first good thing in his life, outside of Annie, walk right out the door with so little a fight the soldier in him was ashamed. Instead of drowning his sorrows in the bottle, he'd submerged them with his tears. Hot tears of grief for the men whose lives had been lost, guilt for the role he'd played in their deaths, and anger that no one had blamed him. No one but himself. After leaving the war zone, he'd visited the families of each of the three men. Not only did they not yell or scream at him, they'd forgiven him.

Despite countless hours of self-reflection, he couldn't understand their forgiveness. If anyone ever played a part in something bad happening to Annie…

Annie. She was the reason he kept holding on despite the blackness in his heart and soul. Her innocence and love gave him hope that maybe, just maybe, he could be redeemed even though he didn't see how. And now Melodie, in her quiet reserved nature and smile that cut through all his bullshit, had found a way to bring a little more light into the darkness.

He'd left the hotel room that afternoon with a purpose. He would find Melodie and give her the explanation she'd asked for. Even if she wouldn't give him another chance to pursue whatever it was they were starting, he'd still tell her the truth. He owed her that. Maybe through dealing with his grief, he could help her deal with her own.

Thankfully, Melodie had mentioned at least the geographical area of Chicago she lived in, and he'd operated under the assumption she worked in the same area. Risky, but gotta start somewhere. With no cell phone number or address to go from, he sketched together a plan from her name, occupation, and his one additional detail. She'd told him she lived in the southwest suburbs of Chicago.

He'd hopped on the first flight to Chicago and checked in to the airport hotel. After several hours of quality time with Google, YP.com, and his cell phone, he'd found her. His enigma worked at the library in Bolingbrook, tucked nicely between three other similar suburbs. A forty-five minute commute later, he stepped inside the brick walls of the library. His pulse quickened when the breathtaking emerald of her eyes once again streamed into his line of vision. God, how he'd missed them. Missed her.

Mesmerized children sat in a semi-circle around Melodie, her expressions and tone of voice transported everyone, including him, to a world of giants, kings, princesses, and happily-ever-afters. Hell, she could read him a bedtime story every night. *Wearing sexy lingerie, of course.* Her voice provided the background noise for the fantasy playing out in his head. As his other head grew impatient for the story to end so he could make his apology, he tucked the daydream safely under the covers until he could revisit it again or, preferably, replace it with the flesh-and-blood woman sitting across the room.

The last page turned as the fairy tale ending neared. He stepped from behind the bookshelf, doubling as cover, and joined in her final words, "And they lived happily ever after."

Visions of Melodie surrounded by miniature replicas of her...or him created an odd sense of peace deep within his soul. Her eyes locked with his for a moment before exuberant children with pent-up energy from sitting so long rushed the little stage to topple her with hugs and squeals of joy.

Incredibly beautiful, warm, caring, and vibrant. His insides vibrated with longing, the need to hold her in his arms and to promise her they'd find a way to put their troubled pasts behind them rendered him momentarily speechless. The arrival of the parents to claim their children snapped him from his thoughts.

Only one little girl remained. "Miss Melodie?"

"Yes, Nessa?"

"Who is he?" The red-haired little girl with bright eyes hidden behind blue-framed glasses pointed in his direction.

Not wanting to give Melodie a chance to explain, he made the strides necessary to put him squarely in front of the little girl. Crouching down, he offered his best smile. Leaning in, he whispered, "Can you promise to keep a secret?"

Wide eyes blinked as her head nodded in agreement.

"I'm her knight in shining armor."

Nessa gasped and covered her mouth, "You are?"

"Yes, ma'am."

"Are you two gonna live happily ever after?"

He chanced a quick look at Melodie, wide-eyed and looking as interested in the answer as Nessa. "Well, young lady, there's a big giant—like the one after Jack—trying to keep us apart. I'm going to do everything in my power to vanquish the bad guy and rescue milady. Can I count on you for help, if needed?" He leveled a wannabe-serious glare at Nessa. At that moment, he was very thankful for all the bedtime stories he'd read to Annie.

Her face wrinkled, scrunching her tiny nose in an adorable fashion. "I'm only six. You're on your own, mister."

He hung his head, hands over his heart. "I shall try to be brave then."

Nessa giggled. "You're silly." She caught sight of her mother and ran toward her. "Bye, Miss Melodie. Bye, Mr. Knight."

Melodie's smile disappeared, the sadness returning to her face. "I'm surprised to see you. I...I didn't think I'd ever see you again."

"I know. You presented a bit of a challenge to find too. I'm sorry about what happened, but I want to talk. What time do you get off?"

"In about fifteen. How'd you find me?"

Her curious nature served as the opportunity to convince her to talk. "Let me buy you dinner, and I'll explain everything."

"Coffee and dessert."

"Drinks?" Threads of desperation seeped into his tone, both alarming and aggravating him. This woman had a way of knocking him off balance every time they spoke.

The familiar site of chocolate brown waves swishing over her shoulders eased the momentary frustration. "I need caffeine." She directed a pointed look squarely at him. "Haven't been sleeping well the past few days."

"Coffee it is." Don't sell past the yes. Good advice his father reminded him of countless times when he was younger.

Thirty minutes later, they were seated at a nearby Starbucks, a triple nonfat latte for her, and black coffee for him, with matching chocolate chip cookies sitting between them.

"How did you find me?"

Straight to the point. I like a woman who doesn't play games. "I made a lot of calls to libraries in the past day or so."

"Why did you find me?"

"Because you left before we could finish our conversation. I've had some time to think, and I'd like the opportunity to explain."

She sipped the hot beverage, watching him through long dark lashes. "I'm sorry I left so abruptly. I...I felt...I don't even know how to explain it. Generally, I'm not that quick to react."

"You were upset. I get it. Now you've had some time to think, can we talk?" Please God, let her be willing to talk about this. He needed to put this behind him and move forward.

A piece of cookie found its way to her mouth as she nodded. He tried hard to remain focused. Nice to know her ability to distract him hadn't diminished.

A slow, deep breath helped him continue. He looked around to see who else might hear his confession. Thankfully, there was only one other patron having their coffee inside, and she was on the other side of the café. "I thought a lot about what you said that morning. I want to tell you what happened."

She took his hand, sending a jolt of warmth through his limbs. "I really do want to know."

He took a deep breath, squeezed her hand, and nodded. "I volunteered for the assignment. One of the locals, who I'd come to know and had fed me and my unit information about rebel activity when I was an enlisted man, had been kidnapped by a faction. He was being held in a remote village. His family hired my company for a rescue attempt. We took two trucks. The first one, manned by three men in uniforms, contained supplies. We wanted it to look like a humanitarian mission in case we were being watched. The second vehicle, my truck, had the weapons."

He released her hand, leaned back in his chair, and closed his eyes. "Everything had been going according to plan when we came to a fork in the road. Both roads led to the same place and, according to the map, were essentially the same distance. The only notable difference was the towns each traversed along the way. The intel in my briefing package revealed no significant threat difference between the two routes. I had to choose."

He opened his eyes. "I had to make a choice—left or right." He exhaled, blinking back the few tears he'd not managed to get rid of. "I chose wrong, and the first truck in the convoy hit the buried bomb not even half a mile down the road. Those three men lost their lives that day because of the decision I made."

The tears bathing her beautiful cheeks almost broke his resolve not to cry. Wanting to feel close to her again, he covered her hand with his. "I thought I'd accepted my role in the incident after my time with the shrink. After you left, I yelled, screamed, even cursed God and everybody wishing this had never happened or that I could just forget about it and move on. In the end, though, I decided I needed to talk about it at least once more. Because of what you went through with Tom, you are the person I wanted to tell. So many brave men and women lost their lives over there. I want you to find peace, even if I'm not at that point yet."

The coffee cup sat forgotten as her gaze pierced his. She was still here, listening intently, so he decided to finish.

"You have to believe that Tom's death had meaning. He died serving his country and trying to help the people in a country ravaged by war. It doesn't make it any easier, but I hope someday you can see the honor in the choices he made. On the other hand, I would give anything to go back and make a different choice—right instead of left."

Her gaze sharpened. He could almost see her mind focus. After several long, painstaking moments, she finally spoke. "It might not have made a difference."

"What?"

"You're assuming there weren't any mines on the other road."

Damn, she's right. He slumped back, his mind begrudgingly reliving the fateful day. "I...I'd never really considered it. The shrink and I focused primarily on the aspect of my survival and the resulting guilt. The subject that either direction might've had the same results never surfaced." If he were still in the military, he'd demand that Lieutenant lose a few stripes.

The silence stretched between them as the information soaked through layers of guilt, denial, and hurt.

"You forgive me?" He needed to know. Her forgiveness was the main reason he'd gone to all this trouble to find her again.

She shook her head, sending a spark of pain straight to the center of his heart. He truly didn't know how he'd ever find another woman who affected him as intensely as the woman sitting across from him. *Or how I'll find peace.*

"There's nothing you need forgiveness for from me. You need to forgive yourself."

"Yeah, well, that's easier said than done." The last thing he needed was someone else psychoanalyzing him.

"I understand. Truly, I do. I've been angry at Tom for leaving me and for getting himself killed. Your words have challenged me to rethink all of it from a different perspective. Rather than focus on his death, I'll focus on his bravery and sacrifice."

She stood, and his heart paused its beating. She was going to leave, and he'd be alone...again. "Let's get out of here," Melodie's hand extended toward him.

The wild thumping in his chest signaled his heart still worked. His inability to read her at this moment both perplexed and excited him. Was his shy librarian taking charge? Yeah, she definitely would be the death of him. But what a way to go.

"Where do you want to go?" He smiled. "I'd suggest my place, but since I checked out of the hotel this morning, that's not really an option."

"You really are a fly-by-the-seat-of-your-pants kind of guy, aren't you?"

At her teasing, he hoped he hadn't misread her signals. He cupped her cheek, pulling her into a kiss. God, how he'd missed those lips. Soft, sexy, and sensual. She resisted at first—a move he totally expected from his cautious librarian. He may not know how to deal with all this psychological bullshit, but he knew how to kiss a woman. A soft *mmmm* from her confirmed his confidence in those abilities. Sliding his tongue over coffee-laden lips, he deepened their connection. The ache in his heart lessened each time he touched her and minimizing pain made the top of the priority list. He'd been right. Melodie provided a much better solution than alcohol. Blocking out all other thoughts, he concentrated on her smooth skin, intoxicating subtle scent, and the sinfully seductive sounds of her pleasure. The world could explode around him right now, and he wouldn't give a damn.

Finally, she pulled away, staring at him from dark emerald eyes. "My place."

CHAPTER TWENTY-TWO

———

Her hands trembled with the key as conflicting emotions, desire, and nerves waged a fierce battle in the forefront of her brain. Since returning from Texas, her world had transformed from black to grey and then somewhere in between as she found her courage to try again. Daniel's surprise visit to the library confirmed her faith in romantic gestures and, maybe, in love itself. Too much of her life had been wasted. No more time for regrets. No more living in Evelyn's shadow. No more avoiding life when it was standing right in front of her—looking incredibly handsome.

"Finally," she chuckled when the lock gave way, and the door opened. "Don't mind the mess. I wasn't expecting company and…"

Her words were cut off as Daniel swept her into his arms and carried her down the short hall. "Is the bedroom this way? I hope you didn't make the bed this morning because I intend to unmake it in grand fashion."

"I…" she yelped as he dropped her unceremoniously onto the queen-size bed which, as he'd hoped, remained unmade.

"I've missed you." His hands slid under her blouse, lifting until the material blocked her vision for a few moments before joining the T-shirt she'd slept in last night. Not even bothering to unfasten her bra, his fingers slid under the silk, exposing her to his gaze and, most importantly, his fiery touch.

"Daniel…mmmm…missed you too." She arched her back as the warmth of his mouth suckled the enervated tip. "Sweet heaven."

His hands deftly unbuttoned, unzipped, and undressed her bottom half. "I plan on taking you so high you have to look down to see heaven."

Sitting up, she reached for him, tugging on the waistband of his shirt to free it from his jeans. "You're overdressed."

"Looking to change that?"

Her hands slid over his muscled chest, nails scraping against his flat nipples. Adrenaline surged at his sharp gasp from her bold move. "Like that?" she whispered. She certainly liked being strong with him and for him.

She gasped as he lifted her off the bed. Her legs wrapped around his waist as strong hands cupped her bottom, holding her close.

"I love it."

His words slipped past any remaining objections her heart might offer. He moved their bodies until her back encountered the paneled wall of the bedroom, delightfully trapping her between two very hard surfaces. The prominent bulge of his denim-covered arousal taunted and teased her satin-clad center. "You're still overdressed."

"Patience, my sexy wallflower. I have to admit, you look pretty damn good pressed up against this particular wall."

She had no chance to reply as his teeth nipped at the sensitive skin behind her earlobe. Heat pulsed and fanned across her flesh, warming her entire being. Fingertips pressed into her thighs, holding her immobile against the short thrusts of his lower body. "Daniel...please."

The moment he released her legs and she regained her balance, she pushed him backward until he fell onto the bed. This time need alone hurried her movements, driving her actions. The button and zipper on his jeans dealt with, she tugged until lean, muscled thighs appeared. "Condom?"

"Wallet," he grunted as she finished undressing him.

A quick scavenger hunt through the pile of clothes revealed the desired object. Moments later, he was ready. She'd been ready since they opened the front door.

"Shit, you're sexy." His eyes swept across her body, burning her skin from the intensity of his gaze. She loved the way he looked at her and made her believe she was the most desirable woman on earth.

Leaning forward she whispered, "Time to deliver on your promise of heaven."

CHAPTER TWENTY-THREE

———

Warmth and a blissful fatigue settled throughout her soul. Her smile had to be more than a "the cat who got the cream" smile. She guessed it registered along the lines of a "the cat who stole the cream and drank every last drop" kind of contented smile. He'd probably gloat, but the smile wouldn't be tamed. Besides, he'd earned a little gloating.

"What's the smile for?" Daniel kissed her damp forehead.

"Admiring the view. You certainly delivered on your promise. Heaven is even more beautiful from this vantage point than I'd imagined."

His fingers cupped her chin and brought her mouth to his for a gentle kiss. "Almost as beautiful as you."

"So, where do we go from here?" The spontaneity of the moment past, she was eager to know where her relationship with him was headed.

"Bathroom?" He moved from the bed with surprising grace and ease.

Her eyes were drawn to the long, toned lines of his body. She was in so much trouble. "Out the door, second room to your right."

He kissed her forehead. "Be right back."

Not exactly what she'd meant by her question, but there'd be time to talk about what their future might look like later. Her stomach rumbled as she stretched. Food needed to factor in the plans for the immediate future. *And after that?* She sat up and tucked her knees in close, hugging herself. The action intensified the pleasure still humming through her body. She might never get enough of quality time with Daniel. Even their arguments invigorated her spirit and made each and every one of her senses come alive. He was wild where she was safe, spontaneous where she was routine, and unpredictable where she was steady. Could two opposites strike a balance?

He returned a few minutes later with a warm cloth and tossed it in her direction.

"Such a gentleman. Thank you. I'm thinking pizza should be next on the agenda."

His focus rested on her dresser where various pictures, folded clothes, and a few days' worth of mail were lined nicely in organized stacks. Picking up the shirt on top of the clothing pile, he turned and winked. "I've been looking for this shirt. Were you planning on returning it at any point?"

She grabbed her bra from the floor and the shirt from his grasp and slid into both with practiced ease. "It looks better on me."

She blushed as his eyes darkened. "It sure does. Alright, you win. You can keep it."

"Like anything special on your pizza?" She dialed the local pizza joint.

"Any meat is good. No veggies."

"Some veggies."

"Fine, green pepper."

After placing the order, she slipped on a pair of shorts and grabbed a couple of sodas from the fridge. She occupied the recliner, while he made himself comfortable on the couch. The whole scenario screamed cozy married couple. She fought the instinct to ask, "So, honey, how was your day?" *For the first time, I can see myself as part of a couple.* A subtle warmth filled her veins and washed over her with a feeling of contentment.

"What's the grin for?" Daniel moved piles of books around on the coffee table to find the remote.

"Not sure. I feel like an old married couple on date night. Sex followed by pizza and television time together."

He stretched out the length of the couch and patted the area in front of him, inviting her to share the space. "Not quite an old married couple yet."

"You sure there's room for both of us." Even as she asked, she moved over to the couch, lying next to him. He adjusted them until her body was half reclined over his.

"See, plenty of room." Daniel pulled her close and snuggled in tight. "I love holding you in my arms. There's something so…"

"Comfortable."

"Yes, comfortable."

Her head resting on the pillow of his chest offered the strangest sense of peace. She wanted to stay like this forever. Not wanting to ruin such a perfect moment, but unable to not know the answer, she tilted her head toward his. "How long can you stay?"

"How long do you want me to stay?"

Forever.

"I guess that depends on what you're looking for in a relationship with me. A friend? A bed buddy? A place to stay when you come to town?" *Someone more permanent in your life?*

"All of the above." The arrogant smile returned with a vengeance.

Her heart clenched in tandem with her jaw. She pushed against his chest and made a move to distance her body. Stirrings of doubt that Daniel could ever be involved in a long-term relationship erased the comfort and contentment of a few moments ago. "So, I'm better than a one-night stand, but you only want to be with me on an as-needed basis?" She fought against the rising heat of anger. "After everything that happened in Texas and you finding me, I thought you wanted more from life…more for us."

He grabbed her hand and pulled her body close to his again. "Hey, hey. Relax. I swear, you really need to learn to calm down, or you're going to have a heart attack at a very young age. Are you always this quick to jump to conclusions?"

Jerking her hand back, she moved to sit on the opposite end of the couch. "Only where you're concerned." *Why is that?* This man not only found but pushed every single button she owned, both good and bad.

"Look. I flew all the way here, played private investigator, and gave you a beautiful view of heaven. Doesn't that at least say I'm interested in a relationship?"

"The question is what kind of relationship?"

Saved by the bell. She made it off the couch, grabbed her purse to pay the delivery guy, and then carried the pizza into the kitchen.

Daniel followed close behind. "Paper plates?"

"Cabinet on the right, on top of the regular plates."

Their discussion on hold, Melodie filled glasses with ice as Daniel cleared the table from a week's worth of newspapers, flyers, and more mail. His recycling job halted, he held up an invitation for her inspection. "Sorry, almost tossed this by accident."

Without even seeing the writing, the embossed cardstock provided her all the information she needed to know. She put a large slice of the Chicago deep-dish pizza on his plate and served herself before grabbing the card and tossing it in the bin. "You like Parmesan or crushed red pepper?"

"No thanks. Why'd you throw that away? It was an invitation to a dinner and reception honoring your sister."

She busied herself with a too-large bite of the cheese and crust goodness, taking her time before answering. "I'm not going."

"Why not?" He followed her example and bit off a large piece, several strands of melted cheese connecting the portion in his mouth to the piece still in his hands.

"Because the thought of another family get together honoring my big sis is more than I can handle right now. We'd begin with how wonderful and successful she is, lauding her latest accomplishment, followed closely by their attempts to hook me up with the latest eligible bachelor. And, lest I forget, mother would finish off the night with another lecture on how if I'd just apply myself and get a real job..."

"Take me as a date."

The soda left her mouth in projectile fashion at his offer. She blushed and grabbed a dish towel to wipe up the resulting mess. "What do you mean?"

He grinned. "You know, guy accompanies girl to family shindig. Guy is incredibly handsome and full of Southern charm. Guy keeps family from picking on girl all evening. Guy brings girl home and gets laid as girl's way of saying thank you."

She couldn't help herself. Her laughter filled the room. "You're very sweet and very much a Southern gentleman. Well, most of the time. I couldn't ask you to do that though."

He pulled her onto his lap and kissed her soundly, making her forget all about the pizza, spilled soda, and family get-togethers. "You didn't ask. I'm offering. " His hand slid down her arm to her waist and under the T-shirt to cup her breast. "Let me do this for you. Think of the fun we'll have."

If he kept touching her like this, she'd skip the party for the sole purpose of staying in bed with him. She nodded. "I'll try to not let them intimidate me if you won't either." The tingling swirled low in her abdomen. Could she be addicted to sex with this man? A mental note added sex addiction to the "to be researched" list.

"Besides, I'd like to meet your sister and see what all the fuss is about." Daniel stood, slipping his arm under her legs to carry her, for the second time that evening, to the still unmade bed.

CHAPTER TWENTY-FOUR

———

The alarm playing a canned jingle woke him from the most pleasant of dreams. The aroma of lilacs permeated his senses and added to the warm feeling of contentment settling deep in his bones this morning. Melodie in his arms, the best part of waking up, no matter what Folgers wanted him to believe. He brushed strands of hair away from her cheek and feathered a kiss across her lips. "Good morning, beautiful."

"Mmmm, not a fan of mornings." She turned in his arms and kissed him sleepily. "Especially when someone kept me up most of the night."

"Didn't hear you complaining, unless you count calling out to a higher being repeatedly your cry for help."

She smacked him on the arm before granting him another kiss. A moment later the covers were tossed, and she got out of bed.

Already he missed her heat.

"I'm not complaining about being kept up. I'm complaining about having to get up."

"You can't call in sick?"

"I just returned from vacation. Can't take any more time off right now. First the funeral. Then my trip..."

He jumped out of bed and put his arms around her. "Shit. I'm sorry, Mel. Didn't mean to bring up bad memories." He didn't want anything he said or did to disturb their little slice of heaven.

She kissed him on the cheek. "I know you didn't. It's going to take time—for both of us. Can you start the coffee while I shower?"

He pulled her close, enjoying the way her body melded against his. Almost as if they were made for each other. "I could shower with you, save time."

Her rich laughter filled the room. "I don't need research to know exactly zero time would be saved. Why don't you take that cute butt of yours into the kitchen and make some coffee?"

Snapping to attention, he saluted and offered his best snarky grin. "Sir! Yes, sir!"

"At ease, soldier. I'll be out in a few."

Being around her kept his "soldier" anything but at ease. A small part of him, though, enjoyed playing house with her. Thirty minutes later, he'd not only made coffee but scrambled eggs and finished off the breakfast with buttered toast. Melodie emerged from the bedroom looking as beautiful as ever in navy slacks and an emerald green blouse that set her eyes off perfectly. Her hair, which looked amazing fanned out over her pillow as her head tossed back and forth in ecstasy, also looked presentable swept to the side in a loose braid.

"You made breakfast too? You really are every woman's dream."

"Tomorrow I'll make French toast. It's my daughter's favorite." He hoped she'd let him stay another night. He watched with delight as she took her first bite.

"Oh sweet Jesus, you put cheese in these." The words purred from her mouth.

Crap, this woman could make eating eggs sexy. "Yeah. Found some cheddar jack in the freezer. Hope that was okay."

"Okay? It's fantastic. Are you secretly a chef too?"

Moving into the chair opposite her, he swallowed some of the strong black brew. If he didn't change the subject, she'd be late for work. "Nah, but when Annie's with me, someone's gotta feed us, right? I've picked up a few things over the years, thanks to her, especially the fact that cheese makes everything better."

"You're a great dad. I can tell from the way your face lights up every time you mention Annie."

He nodded. "She's a great kid. Makes it easier to be a great dad." He clasped his hand over hers. "I'm sure you're going to make a great mom someday too."

Melodie pulled her hand back and picked up the giant mug of coffee. Her eyes flickered with some emotion. Pain? Anger? Remorse? The blinking and coffee mug prevented him from having enough time to dissect the response.

"Thanks." She wiped her mouth and stood. "I should leave for work. Don't want to be late. I have a committee meeting first thing this morning." She leaned over and kissed him, brief and chaste. "What are your plans for today?"

Skillful misdirection. Nice try. "I'm going to drive around and get familiar with the area and do a little shopping since I'm going to a party. What is appropriate attire for arm candy at an Alexander social event?"

The acceleration of his heart when her hand swept across his chest lit fire in his veins. If she remained a part of his life, he could probably do away with caffeine entirely, if the adrenaline didn't kill him first.

"I'm sure whatever you wear will be perfect." She leaned nearer, the heat from her body and the soft breath from her whisper sent the recently lit fire straight to his groin.

Yes, without a doubt, going to kill him.

"Just know it will never compare to the flesh and blood that rests beneath the clothes." She leaned over and kissed him. "There's a spare key in the pink bowl on the counter so you can get back in."

The warmth of her kiss vanished when the door closed. He was alone. Alone with the dishes and his thoughts. *I don't deserve her. Don't deserve this.* Melodie had walked him to an emotional cliff, and he jumped off without looking, without so much as a damn parachute. Now, here he was playing domestic goddess and shopping for party clothes. What the hell had happened to him?

The sexy librarian. That was what happened. Her reserved, cautious manner called out to his deep, protective nature. Though perfectly capable of handling herself, she opened up and shared her vulnerability. Vulnerable and sexy, a lethal combination for him. Washing up the dishes, he contemplated the upcoming meeting with her family. Was this a test? Since Belle, no woman had ever taken him home to meet the family. Once again he'd jumped off without looking. He'd offered to meet the family, and he still didn't have the woman's damn cell phone number. Hopefully, the ground would be soft when he hit the bottom 'cause he sure as hell couldn't stop his descent.

The dishes done, he grabbed some clean clothes from his duffel bag and hit the shower. The water offered little relief from the growing pressure in his chest. He rubbed the back of his neck to ease the tightness. Old demons clawing their way into his happiness. Would Melodie use him as countless other women had? The sex was good, friggin' amazing even. They'd both been pretty honest about the baggage they brought into the relationship—at least he assumed she'd done the same. There'd been a flash of something when he mentioned her being a great mom. Maybe she'd had an abortion or given a child up for adoption when she was younger? That aside, the surprise at his offer to accompany her to the event seemed genuine, but he'd been fooled by less beautiful and intriguing women.

Could Melodie be different? He considered the possibility the innocence might be an act she'd honed over the years. The cooling water renewed his resolve. Cause and effect. He'd find the best damn outfit, be a Southern gentleman, and prove he could be everything she needed. If the big bad wolf emerged from innocent red riding hood's cloak, he'd pack up and leave.

Or…if she turned out to be every bit as wonderful as he believed she was, he'd fight his biggest enemy—himself—to justify his right to this kind of happiness. He sighed. The second choice may prove the most difficult.

Turning off the stream of water, he rested his forehead against the wet tile. The constant battle of worthiness that raged inside his soul drained the energy from his body. The relationship game never ended in his favor, which was why he'd stopped playing. Despite his ability to lie to others, he couldn't lie to himself. If he couldn't make this work with Melodie, he'd never make it work with anyone.

CHAPTER TWENTY-FIVE

———

"Tell me more." Lydia's voice carried louder than appropriate for a library.

"Shhh! Lower your voice before you draw the attention of every person in a three block radius, including our boss."

Lydia's dark black hair swayed as she nodded in agreement from the other side of the shelf. A couple of thick books were removed, and her spectacle-framed blue eyes came into view. "Sorry, but this is a fairy tale worthy story, and you're the main character. I've been married for fifteen years to the same man, living in suburban Chicago with two-point-three kids and a dog. My life needs a little excitement."

The sparkle in Lydia's eyes was contagious, and Melodie couldn't help but share in her enthusiasm. "This is so unlike me. It feels…weird." *And exhilarating all at the same time. I've fallen…fallen hard.*

"Nice word choice," the older woman laughed as she moved more books around.

She sighed. Daniel had that effect on her. "He defies explanation. My reaction to him defies explanation. He's taken every protective wall I've built around myself and effectively knocked them over with a battering ram."

"He's at your house right now?"

"He was there when I left." Fear gripped her heart. Would he be there when she returned? Ugh, this was worse than high school dating.

"Are you going to move to Mississippi to be with him?" Lydia finished restocking her shelf and joined Melodie on her side to assist.

"Move? I guess I haven't thought that far ahead. I only met him a little over a week ago. I can't pick up my entire life and move away from my family for a man I met last week."

"Now, all of a sudden, you're worried about being away from your family? I thought you couldn't stand to be around them."

"I can't. Well, except my dad. I'd miss him." She'd always been close with her dad. They'd been ports of safe haven for each other in the crazy storm of ambition her mother and sister generated as easily as they breathed.

"Your father would want you to be happy."

Did Daniel make her happy? Equal parts happiness and misery so far. "I don't know. He has to survive the first family get together, and we'll go from there."

"You should call and check in. See how he's doing. Let him know you're thinking of him. My husband always loves that, even if he won't admit it to any of his buddies."

"I…" She stopped.

"What?"

"Damn."

"Melodie?"

She sat on the step stool, a stack of books resting on her lap, chuckled, and looked at her coworker and friend. "I still don't have his cell number."

Lydia leaned up against the wall of books. "Let me get this straight. You meet this man and go on a couple of dates, which include staying out all night. You invite him to your hotel room, he shows up at your place of business, you invite him back to your place and have mind-blowing sex—several times, I might add. He makes you breakfast and offers to rescue you from a family social event, and you still don't have his cell number?"

Melodie's eyes closed as the irony of the situation washed over her. "No. No, I don't."

Lydia's laughter filled the air, prompting a shushing from somewhere in the room. "I suggest you remedy that little issue tonight as soon as you get home."

"I will, I promise. Now help me finish putting away these books before I lose my job and have to move back in with my parents."

"Or with Daniel…" The idea hung in the air around the top shelf of the self-help books.

"Let it go." She couldn't think that far ahead. She wanted to, but her heart needed a break from relationship pain, so one slow step at a time.

Lydia sighed dramatically. "Fine, but I want to see a picture soon. Old gals need to have fantasy material, you know."

She nudged the woman. "You're not old, and your husband is a dream."

"Yeah, yeah. Back to work."

Melodie forced her thoughts back to the Dewey Decimal system and prayed Daniel's presence in her life turned out to be more than a dream.

CHAPTER TWENTY-SIX

———

"Daniel? Are you still here?" Her sweet voice filtered into the living room where he'd spent the last hour or so waiting for her return, while thumbing through the countless cable channels.

"In here. Your television channels suck, by the way." He patted the area next to him on the couch. "How was work?"

She grabbed the beer from his hand and took a quick swig before settling in next to him and tucking her feet underneath her legs. "I never watch television, and the kids in the after-school reading group were wired today. How was shopping?"

"I found something presentable. Thought I'd wear it to dinner tonight for your approval. While I was out shopping, I found a great restaurant to try inside the Bass Pro Shop."

Her nose wrinkled in an adorable fashion. "A restaurant inside the Bass Pro Shop? You catch it—we cook it kind of deal?"

"Not exactly. The menu looked great and I've been jonesing for some good seafood. We have six o'clock reservations so you need to shower and change."

"Do I smell?"

He buried his nose in the curve of her neck, inhaling her scent. She wore lilac, and it suited her well.

Not sure that it mattered, but he prided himself on noticing details. "You smell delicious, but I figured you'd want a shower to freshen up."

Her leg swung over his lap, straddling his lower body. "Want to freshen up with me?"

This woman served equal parts of shy and seductress. "As tempting as that sounds, I have other plans for tonight."

Disappointment settled over her rosy cheeks. "For the entire night?"

His hands slid to her neck and pulled her pouting lips to his for a steal-your-breath kind of kiss. He wanted to join her in the shower...in the bed...hell, even against the wall again, but he wanted something more from tonight—from this relationship. "Let's have dinner, talk, and then we'll see where the rest of the evening takes us. Deal?"

She stood, dropping the temperature in the room a few degrees, and prompted him to rethink his plans for tonight. *Be responsible. Long-term goals.* He'd made himself a deal to change his focus from short-term to long-term plans after wallowing in self-pity for the better part of the day. Earlier, doing the right thing pumped his chest with pride. With Melodie straddling his body, offering a wild night of sex, other areas of his body pumped in response. Yeah, being responsible sucked.

"What do you want to talk about?"

He swatted her behind and somehow managed to ignore her perfect ass. "Get ready, woman. I don't like being late."

Thirty minutes later, he whistled as she stepped into the living room. *Find the right words. Damn, she looks good.* He didn't bother much with fashion, brand names, and styles as he was a minimalist—the less clothing women wore, the better. A straight black skirt with strappy high heels provided the backdrop for an emerald blouse. Satin, if he had to guess. The color highlighted her eyes and made them even more beautiful, if that was possible. "Very classy."

She smiled at his compliment and gestured to her outfit. "What? This old thing?"

He pulled her into a kiss, wanting to show her with actions, where he knew words would fail him. His tongue swept across her ruby lips before tasting the peppermint of her toothpaste. As her hands slid up and down his back, he started to dismiss the idea of dinner. Then her stomach rumbled.

"Hungry?"

The blood in his body heated a few degrees as her hands slid up his crisply pressed, dark navy shirt. "Mmmm, but I'm not sure if it's more for dinner or dessert. You look pretty handsome yourself, by the way."

Stepping back, he struck a model pose. "What? This old thing?"

For his effort, he received a punch in the arm. "The old thing you bought earlier today?"

Taking her hand, he grabbed her purse and handed it to her. "Yes, the very one. Now let's go before they give our reservations away."

"Wait!" Melodie stopped and pulled out her cell phone. "Before we do one more thing together, I want your cell number."

"Are you sure you're ready for that level of commitment? That means I can call or text whenever I want." He let his fingers slide down her porcelain cheek.

She took his phone and handed hers over so he could input his information. His fingers trembled as he typed in the digits, a slight sheen of perspiration covering them. She represented the third woman he'd ever given his number to. First Belle, then Alana, and now Melodie. He handed her phone back, a little damper than when she turned it over. Was *he* ready for this level of commitment?

* * *

"Well, as much as I hate to admit it, dinner here ranked pretty high on the places I'd like to eat again list."

Daniel patted his belly. "Food and women, two things I know a lot about."

"I won't argue with you on the food but an expert on women? I might challenge you on that point, sir."

He leaned in, elbows on the table, blue eyes searching for something…something deep within her soul. "Now that I've been totally honest with you, I want you to be honest with me. There's something in those beautiful eyes of yours, a hesitation that tells me there's something more than your family dynamics and Tom's death that is causing you pain." He offered a small smile. "Now that we've exchanged cell numbers and taken our relationship to a more involved level, I think we should put all our cards on the table."

His words sent in the troops responsible for lifting the gates around her heart, putting her immediately on guard. "Exchanging cell numbers gives you the right to ask personal questions? So much for your almighty knowledge on women."

Large hands captured hers and pulled her closer. She did a quick check to make sure her blouse wasn't soaking up any of the leftovers on her plate. Once the material proved safe, she had no choice but to find his gaze again. Dread filled the remaining space left in her stomach. What could he possibly ask? *Very few secrets. Only one.*

"Since I've only given my number to two other women, for me it means something."

For only a moment, she allowed herself to think this made her special, but then she remembered. The memory pierced her heart with reality. "Makes sense. If you were only interested in a one-night stand, why bother with exchanging numbers. Use 'em and lose 'em, right?"

His eyes flashed and darkened. "Damn it, woman, you have more security and defense strategies built around your heart than Bin Laden and Saddam put together."

Reflection and redirection represented two of the primary weapons in her arsenal for the ongoing battle against her mother and sister. Old habits were hard to break. Yet Daniel had broken a couple of his habits by spending more than one night with her and sharing his cell number. "I'm sorry. I'm not the sharing type. For what it's worth, I've shared more with you than anyone else…ever."

Daniel ignored both her avoidance and her admission. "Tell me why those gorgeous eyes of yours get haunted every time the subject of children comes up."

She pulled her hands away, the subject too painful—too fresh—too devastating. *It was painful for him to share, yet he did.* "I really don't like talking about it. Can we go home now?" Lifting one hand, she signaled the waiter for the check.

Daniel moved her plate aside before recapturing her hands. "After everything we've shared with each other, secrets from the past, I can't imagine this being any worse."

A renegade tear escaped and moistened her cheek. Not wanting him to see her cry again, she wiped the tear away and leveled a sad look in his direction. "You wouldn't be able to imagine, as you are both a man and a father."

The waiter arrived and halted conversation. Daniel immediately pulled out his card and placed it on the tiny tray with the bill, not even looking at the amount. "You have a lot of preconceived notions about men."

"Cause and effect, remember?" She wanted this night to be over. She'd been wrong. Daniel's larger-than-life presence was too much for her quiet and reclusive ways.

The waiter returned, and Daniel signed the check. "Ready to go?"

Mutely she nodded, ignoring the irritation oozing from every pore of his muscled and well-toned being. Not telling him was the right thing, she was sure. None of his business. She'd told no one her secret, certainly not her family. Once they knew...Once he knew...

The ride home transpired in silence. Several times she started to tell him. Her mouth opened and then closed, unable to find the right words to explain. Maybe more than words, it was fear that kept her from sharing. Fear that whatever they had would be over. Finally, they arrived back at her place after she'd endured the longest fifteen minutes of her life. For some unexplainable reason, her heart somersaulted in her chest when he followed her inside. He was staying.

Time to try to salvage this night. "Coming to bed? I know the cable channels suck, but I'm sure I can find some way to entertain you."

He kissed her cheek.

Not a good sign.

"I'm going to grab a pillow and crash on the couch tonight, if it's still alright I stay."

Her eyes blinked rapidly as her muscles tightened, requiring a concerted effort not to tremble in front of him. She didn't want him to leave. Even more so, she wanted him to stay. "Of course you can stay. Where else would you go?" *Please don't say home. Please don't say home!*

Broad shoulders shrugged. "Wouldn't be the first night I've spent in a hotel."

She forced her voice to stay calm and even. "No need. You can stay here and," she reached out and put her hand tentatively over his heart, wanting...needing to touch him, "sleep wherever you're most comfortable. Besides, if you leave, you'll never know what kind of breakfast I'm capable of serving."

Focus became difficult as her eyes were drawn to his fingers, the same ones responsible for so much of her pleasure over the past twenty-four hours. Her hand dropped as she watched him unbutton his shirt. She swallowed hard when his six-pack came into view. Desire pulsed low in her abdomen as his pants followed, leaving only the black boxers. Images of his beautiful body moving over her flooded her mind, prompting her to squeeze her legs together a little tighter to ease the ache building at an unbearable level with each innocent—or not so innocent—movement.

He slid onto the couch, the long lines of his body decorating her cushions better than any pillow or throw she could purchase. "I'm most comfortable right here. Good night, Mel." His hand reached for the remote.

The longing and need in every feminine part she possessed demanded she try one more time. "Why won't you come to bed?"

His eyes locked on hers, the gaze flat and unemotional. "Cause and effect."

CHAPTER TWENTY-SEVEN

———

It wasn't even ten on a Friday night, and he was in bed. Hell, not even in bed. On a couch—a cold, lonely couch. It was his own damn fault. The woman of his dreams was flipping through the same channels not twenty feet away from him. He adjusted the pillow for the tenth time since he'd sent Melodie away without so much as a proper good night kiss. She'd wanted more—a lot more. They always did. They wanted his body, his money, but not his heart.

He pounded the pillow for good measure. He believed, deep down, Melodie tipped the scales differently than other women. He wanted her to be different…needed her to be different. Muting the volume, he listened for sounds coming from her room. After a few minutes, the dramatic music indicated she'd tuned in to a chick flick. *Women!* It wasn't enough she kept her nose buried in a fictional world. She watched those same stories brought to life on the small screen. No wonder men had a hard time measuring up. Most, if not all, of the men in the books and on television were being written by women. Of course, they'd always say the right thing and get the girl in the end.

He heard the soft pads of her feet coming down the hall before he saw her. Seeing her in his T-shirt and boy shorts ignited all the nerves he'd been trying to calm over the last thirty minutes or so. She walked across the room until she was standing between him and the television. "Got a minute?" She turned and looked at the screen. "Unless you really want to see how the Hallmark movie ends."

Shifting to a sitting position, he grumbled. "I figured that's what you were watching and wanted to see what all the fuss was about."

Taking a seat in the chair on the opposite side of the couch, she reached over and clicked the off button on the remote. "I promise I'll tell you how it ends."

"I'd rather hear about you. You're so much better than make believe." He smiled, wanting to put her at ease. He, of all people, knew how hard it was to share something painful.

She clasped her hands and exhaled slowly. "I want you to know that I've not shared this with anyone else yet. You sharing your cell number with me meant something significant to you. My telling you this means something significant to me. The more I thought about it, the more I realized you deserved to know."

"Just tell me, Mel."

"I can't have children."

He heard her words the same moment he saw a couple tears break free and spill down her cheek. Though he wanted to close the distance between them to comfort her, he wanted to let her share what was weighing on her heart. More tears were glistening, waiting their turn. God, how he hated when women cried. "What do you mean?"

Her hands crossed over her stomach as the tears continued to fall. "I mean I'm physically unable to bear children. I've had female problems almost from the beginning, severe endometriosis. A side effect is infertility."

Screw the wait. She needed him now. He moved off the couch and knelt in front of her to wipe away the tears. She held his hand to her cheek. "I've tried everything that's safe, including any treatments whose side effects weren't worse than the disease. No success."

He pulled her closer and kissed her hair as he murmured words of comfort. "Shhh, don't cry. This is not the end of the world. I care about you. I want more than one night. Hell, I'm not sure a lifetime of one nights would be enough with you. We don't need any more children to be happy. Just you, me, and Annie. That's all we need."

"I'm sorry I didn't tell you at dinner. I'm still trying to adjust to all of this myself."

Standing, he took her hand and pulled her body flush with his. Kissing her forehead, he put his arms around her and held her tight. "I get that. Once the dust settles and, if you want to talk about other options, we will. Just know, this isn't a deal breaker for me."

After several minutes, he heard her muffled voice. "You still want to sleep on the couch?"

He chuckled, swept her into his arms, and carried her toward the bedroom. "Hell no! That couch is lumpy."

Saturday

The smell of coffee brewing tempted his eyelids open. He checked his cell, eight o'clock. The last time he'd looked, the numbers indicated a little after four. Great, nowhere near the recommended eight hours. Of course, he couldn't remember getting eight hours sleep in a very long time. Even though he'd ended up snuggling with Melodie, all of the sharing he'd done of late, and the general turmoil in his life, resulted in nightmares plaguing his sleep. They'd been their worst right after the incident, but he'd managed to bury everything deep enough in his subconscious that the nightmares had been replaced by a general restlessness. Not great, but better than the alternative.

He sniffed the air for any signs of breakfast being cooked. Big breakfasts were a staple at his home growing up. No discernible traces of bacon, eggs, sausage, or even oatmeal. Time for a closer look. "Dressed up a lot for a Saturday morning breakfast, aren't you?" His eyes couldn't help but drink in the perfectly tailored brown pants and ivory silk blouse. When she turned toward him, coffee cup in hand, the jade gems captivated him once again. Would he ever lose interest in those amazing eyes?

"Dress code for work, business casual."

"You have to work today? It's Saturday." His eyes darted around the kitchen for any signs of breakfast, his stomach's rumbling becoming more pronounced with each passing minute.

"Libraries are open on Saturdays and kids are out of school. Perfect time for a children's librarian to be at work. It's only a half-day, so I'll be home in time to change and get ready for the party tonight at five. We'll need to leave around quarter to four as traffic going into the city can be a bear." She hesitated. "You're still planning on coming, right?"

Wanting to reassure her and feel those soft curves in his arms again, he moved next to her and removed her coffee cup, setting it down on the nearby table. He pulled her into a light embrace. "I said I'd be your date, and I will." He moved a wave of hair from her shoulder to expose her neck, placing a small kiss on the soft curve. The familiar lilac infused his senses, and he would forever associate this scent with the one-of-a-kind woman he now held. "You have my cell number," he murmured against her skin. "It means something."

She turned in the embrace, her lips finding his. He loved the feel of satin against his skin. The sensation was almost as pleasant as when their naked bodies were pressed together in the throes of passion—almost. She felt so right in his arms, more so than any other woman. His hands slid lower to cup her perfectly rounded bottom. He wanted her to feel, with no room for misunderstanding, the effect she had on him.

An insistent buzzing pulled her warmth away from him. Damn cell phones. This time, however, hers was the culprit.

"Hello, Mother."

He grinned as she rolled her eyes and moved away from him. "Yes, I'm going to be there tonight."

She opened the pantry and pulled out a box of glazed donuts, setting them in front of him. "No, that won't be necessary. I'm bringing a date."

This was her idea of breakfast? A box of glazed donuts? He might be able to make allowances for all of the baggage they both were bringing into this relationship, but this was bullshit. He opened the box of donuts and put one on the paper plate she'd set out for him before the coffee roused him from sleep.

"Yes, Mother. I know. I'll be sure and bring a proper gift. Yes…good-bye."

As soon as she disconnected, he lifted the donut. "This is your idea of breakfast?"

He forgot about food the moment her lips seared his, branding him with a kiss requiring a cold shower the moment she left for work.

"Yes, I'm a terrible cook. Now you know at least one more of my secrets." She smiled and cupped his cheek, her hand caressing the stubble. "I'll do some research on the cooking issue, but you'll have to be patient with me."

"Patience is my middle name." He kissed her, grateful they'd been able to work through another obstacle on their path to happiness. *Undeserved happiness...* He smiled and patted her on her perfectly rounded bottom. "Now go to work, and tonight we'll be the talk of the party."

"Thank you." She grabbed her travel mug and slipped a donut into a sandwich-size plastic bag.

He smiled at her retreating form, admiring the slight sway of her hips. She truly had no idea the level of sexy she delivered with each step.

"We'll work on the cooking thing!"

* * *

The four hours required of her on a Saturday generally passed by with speed and fun. Today, each minute dragged its feet through deep, wet sand, making each hour elapse slower than a millennia. Equally excited and apprehensive about tonight, the thought of Daniel at her side calmed her. Despite his being an emotional roller coaster, his physical presence grounded her. She hadn't even read more than a few pages in a book after the first days with him. Could his presence in her life mean she no longer wanted to escape reality or at least not for the same reasons?

The first big test in their relationship, a party with her family, would serve as a critical proving ground. If he survived the meal intact and didn't catch the first plane out of O'Hare, maybe they might have a future.

She stepped through the doorway, happiness surrounding her in a comforting blanket. "Honey, I'm home." The singsong nature of her voice was certain to elicit a response from Daniel.

Silence.

"Daniel?" She listened for sounds from the back of the apartment. Nothing. Her eyes darted about the small square footage for evidence of his presence. The pounding in her heart shot off a rapid fire of "I told you so" warnings, even as she made her way to the bedroom.

"Unbelievable." She hurried back to the kitchen, moving the stacks of mail, magazines, and other clutter. No Daniel. No note. Nothing. How could she have been so wrong?

He'd left—without a trace—without a note—without a "thanks for the memories." This screamed low, even for him. Maybe all the secrets they'd shared had been too much. Maybe she really hadn't gotten through to him and convinced him he deserved happiness. Maybe she was destined to lose in the game of love.

His cell number!

Maybe something had happened—something preventing him from keeping his promise. She retrieved her cell. No texts. No voice mails. With shaking fingers, she located his number and initiated the call. Straight to voice mail. "Daniel, its Melodie. I arrived home from work and you're... I hope everything is okay. I'm sure there's a really good explanation for you being a no-show again. I hope...just call me, okay?" *Hope he hasn't broken my heart.*

A litany of reminders paraded through her head, primarily from the women in her family about her inability to pick the right man. Her phone rang. She almost dropped it as she checked the caller ID, unwilling to admit even to herself how much she wanted it to be Daniel calling to explain his bizarre disappearing act.

Mother.

Pressing the ignore button, she sent her straight to voice mail. Now was not the time for instruction, warning, or an "I told you so" from the woman who secretly believed she should've stopped after Evelyn's birth. She turned the phone to silent. With no ringing, she could check the phone for texts, without having to endure the calls from her mother. Her old-time friend, insecurity, nagged at her. Daniel hadn't called the last time he ran off and left her with a heaping dose of disappointment. But they'd both changed, hadn't they? There had to be a plausible reason he hadn't returned. Maybe he'd gone out exploring the area and lost track of time.

Her eyes scanned for signs of his belongings as she slowly walked the length of the apartment. Her hope that he'd just lost track of time fell to the bottom of her wish list when she realized the army green duffel he'd brought was no longer sitting in the corner of the bedroom.

She grabbed a bottle of wine and made her way to the bathroom. An evening with a bottle, bubbles, and a book sounded far better than attending a party. As she turned on the water in the bathtub, she could only hope her old habits of escape would help her forget the man who'd stolen her heart.

CHAPTER TWENTY-EIGHT

———

Sunday

Mornings. Oh how she hated mornings. They were terrible, even if preceded by a soothing night of blissful sleep. Last night ranked painfully low on the sleep scale. The thought of going back to work tomorrow sent a fresh wave of pain through her already aching head. She looked around for some indicator of the time, disappointed to see the numbers displaying a lone ten.

Daniel's disappearance and her normal go-to solutions for dealing with her family left her with an aching heart and head. Even the pages of a book from her favorite author failed to carry her away to a place guaranteed to have a happily ever after.

She needed to check her cell phone again to see if there were any missed calls or texts from Daniel. Of course, that would require her getting out of bed and finding the phone.

The steady pounding on her front door forced her to get up, whether she wanted to or not. "I'm coming!" The increased decibel of her reply created an echoing pounding in her head. Oh, how she hated mornings.

She hesitated before opening the door. What if it was Daniel? She looked like hell. *What if it is? Who cares?*

Disappointment combined with relief blanketed her when a quick check through the peephole revealed the man standing on the other side to be her father. A few moments later, the wooden barrier between them disappeared as she reluctantly opened the door to let him in. *At least it isn't mom.* "Hey, Dad."

Pulled into an abrupt bear hug by the only man who hadn't disappointed her, Melodie let herself be comforted.

"We've been worried sick, baby. I know you hate family functions, but when you didn't show up, didn't answer your phone…"

Guilt stabbed fresh wounds in her heart. She'd been so self-absorbed last night, she didn't stop to consider how much her father would worry. "I'm sorry, Dad. Yesterday ranked pretty high on the crap scale, and I couldn't face mother and Ev, especially at a party. I didn't mean to worry you." The pounding in her head increased triple time as she realized she'd done the same thing to her parents that upset her about Daniel's behavior. "Regardless, I should've called. I really am sorry I worried you."

His embrace grew stronger, and she buried her face in his soft cotton shirt. Inhaling the familiar scent soothed her raw and hurting nerves, "Your mother was worried too."

She looked up and leveled him with her best *I don't believe you* expression. "Aren't we past lying to each other about these things? I'm a big girl and know where I rank on the disappointment scale with mother."

He smiled lovingly, "Well, in all truthfulness, she was angry at first."

"Angry?" You didn't have to make your living surrounded by words to know her father was hedging.

This time the small bevy of wrinkles on his tanned face angled upward as his smile grew. "Okay, livid would be a better adjective."

"Now I believe you." She returned to the pleasant task of basking in her father's attention.

"If you listen to your messages, well, after the first three anyway, you'll find her anger eventually morphed into disbelief and then finally into worry."

Melodie straightened, breaking the embrace. "Yet, here you are instead of her. Is she busy consoling my big sister on the disappointment of not everyone showing up to honor the wonder woman she's become?" Her caustic words darkened the mood in the room further. At this juncture, bitterness represented the best she could offer.

He rubbed his face and shrugged broad shoulders. "Your mother is who she is. We're never going to change that. It doesn't change, however, that she was worried something terrible had happened to you." His gaze turned reproachful. "As was I."

"Why Dad? Why do you stay? I don't need you to tell me what happened. You wanted to come check on me. Mother insisted you not leave the party. I may not be able to get her out of my life. For better or worse, she's my mother, and I continue to be her biggest disappointment."

Her father stood an impressive and still-handsome six feet of gentleman. "Because, baby girl, I promised for better or worse. That means something to me." He kissed her forehead, "I'm glad you're alright."

Five words from her father: *"That means something to me,"* echoed Daniel's promise when they'd discussed the importance of exchanging cell numbers. She steeled herself against the sadness weaving through her heart and lifted her chin. "Not that it makes it any better, but ironically I was dealing with the same worry. My date turned into a no-call, no-show." She pulled him into a hug, "Why can't all men be like you?"

"Because, I'm one-in-a-million."

His attempt at levity worked, easing the tension in her jaw and allowing a small smile.

"That you are."

"I'm also the bearer of bad news."

"That doesn't sound promising." Really? Could today get any worse?

"Once I confirmed you were alive, my job was to deliver instructions ensuring your irresponsible butt is at the dinner table Friday night."

She flopped back on the couch. Without a doubt, she should skip this dinner, excuse or not. But, she wouldn't do that to her father. "So, humble pie for dessert?"

He nodded and winked. "Right after she serves your head on a platter for the main course."

Thoughts of Daniel's head on a platter eased her distress momentarily. As much as she complained about her family, they were still hers, and she needed to take responsibility for her actions. "Great. See you then. Hope you still love me when I'm headless."

One final kiss on her cheek. "I'll love you always. Don't be late or not even I can save you then."

CHAPTER TWENTY-NINE

———

Monday

"Hi, it's Melodie. Leave your name and number, and I'll get back to you as soon as possible."

Thankfully, he'd been able to finish his message before the signal cut out. Hospitals were notorious for sketchy connections. He tossed the phone on the couch. He'd been trying to reach the stubborn woman all afternoon. Her phone was ringing, but the damned service still kept sending him into voice mail hell after five rings. He would've called sooner but figured she was at work. He'd left a note and was surprised she hadn't called him. When his ex-wife's father called to say Annie and her mom had been in a car wreck, he'd vaulted into action. The note had been brief but at least had explained Annie was in trouble, and he had to go.

"Daddy?" The groggy voice of his daughter brought him back to the present nightmare.

"Hey, princess, how are you feeling?" He stroked her bruised face, fighting back tears.

"A little better. Thank you for the teddy bear."

His heart swelled. He loved this little girl so much. "You're welcome. He's almost as big as you. Let me help you get him under the covers so you two can snuggle." He maneuvered the large stuffed animal until safely nestled in her arms.

"Where's Mommy?"

He had no idea how to explain the drinking finally caught up to her. "Mommy's in a different hospital right now and is going to need to stay there for a while."

"Do I have to stay here while she's in the hospital?" Small blue eyes filled with fear.

"No, princess. The doctors say you can leave tomorrow if you continue to do well. You're going to stay with me for a while. You know how you stay with me for a longer time during the summer?"

Her eyes lit up. "Yes."

"Well, Mommy and I talked about it, and you're going to stay with me while she gets better." In truth, Belle had been anything but cooperative. Her father, along with the family attorney, convinced her to cooperate. Though the other driver hadn't been killed, he'd been injured, and Belle faced, minimally, a driving under the influence charge along with a civil suit for damages. The family's money certainly wouldn't hurt her chances, but even they couldn't deny the time involved to sort through the mess. A mess they could no longer push under the rug.

Once the dust settled, filing for temporary sole custody of Annie would be a top priority. He had already planned to take steps toward changing the custody arrangement. This incident prompted him to elevate the timetable. *I fought for my country. Sure as hell going to fight for my little girl.*

"Daddy?"

His attention returned to his daughter. "Yes, baby?"

Her lower lip trembled as tears started to fall. "Will Mommy be mad I'm staying with you?"

"No. Mommy knows she needs to get better and learn how to take care of herself before she can take care of you again. Even your grandfather agrees." He knew Annie understood the final word in any situation rested with her grandfather, the head of the family. Wealth, power, and long-standing Southern tradition ensured this wouldn't change anytime soon.

Annie calmed considerably and settled back into the comfort of the teddy bear, sleep looming close by. "Maybe I can visit her for a little bit in the summer."

He stroked her golden hair. "Maybe, sweetheart…maybe."

Monday Evening

"I'm going to operate under the assumption something has gone horribly wrong with your phone and it no longer functions since you haven't returned any of my calls." He paused, measuring his words carefully. "I didn't want to leave a message before because I'd rather talk to you to explain. But since you haven't called or picked up, I figure this will have to do. Your message said you hoped nothing happened. It did. Not to me, but to my daughter, Annie. I want to explain, but I can't do that if you won't talk to me. C'mon, Mel. You have my number, and that still means something…at least it does to me."

Daniel tossed the phone onto the empty space next to him on the couch and rubbed his face. A quick check revealed Annie still resting comfortably. The doctors had agreed she could be released tomorrow morning after a final exam. Lots of bruises, but those would heal. The lawyers worked out the initial details. Annie would stay at his place in Mississippi for a while. They'd pick up her things in the morning and make the drive to his house. Many details would still need to be addressed, but this was an important first step.

He looked at his phone again, willing it to ring. If she didn't call soon, he and Annie were taking a mini vacation to Chicago before she enrolled in school. She was in second grade. A few days away wouldn't hurt. The trip would give Annie a break from all the drama and one last chance for him to make things right with Melodie. He'd had a lot of time to think during the flight home. Worry over his daughter's situation occupied most of his thoughts, but the random chaos in his head revealed one very important detail. There were no guarantees about what the future held. Things could change in an instant. He'd wasted enough time chasing after women who'd never be a part of his future. He'd be damned if he'd let the only person who'd found her way past every barrier go without a fight.

CHAPTER THIRTY

———

Tuesday

"Call him, already." Lydia's motherly voice echoed loudly in the empty children's section of the library. "You've been moping around, looking like you lost your last friend. He's called you, left a message, and wants to talk. What more do you want from the guy?"

"I did try to return his call last night, but it went directly to voicemail. I went to the arboretum on Sunday after my dad left and after work yesterday. It's so peaceful there, and I needed some quiet time to think. My cell doesn't get any reception so when I got home last night, I listened to his message. That's when I tried but couldn't reach him. I get that he was worried about Annie. I'm worried about her too, and I've never even met her. As for what I want? I don't even know anymore. The man creates so many conflicting emotions in me I can't think straight."

A comforting arm rested across her shoulders. "That's the kind of man you want around for the long haul. Life is never boring with them. He's also the kind of man who's a great father and puts his own wants and needs behind concern for his daughter. In his message he mentioned something happened to Annie, right? I know you aren't a mom yet. God knows your mom isn't the best role model for how parents should behave. Trust me when I say if something happens to your child, you forget everything else until you know they're safe. All I'm saying is when he does explain, try to put yourself in his shoes."

"Am I being selfish and stubborn?" Melodie's defensive tone slipped out, which indicated to her she mostly likely was being at least a little of both.

Lydia squeezed her tighter. "Not selfish. You're in love and you're hurting. Your reaction is understandable."

She wiped away the escaping tear and offered the older woman a half smile. "I noticed you didn't give me a pass on being stubborn."

"I call 'em like I see 'em, girlie. Now, let's finish this so you can go home and call this poor man to sort through the mess you've both created."

Melodie paced her apartment, trying to summon the courage to press the appropriate digits necessary to reestablish the connection with Daniel. She didn't know what it was about his arrogant, cocky, sexy, and sweet disposition that not only unnerved her but also made her feel gloriously alive. Exhaling a purposeful breath, she willed her fingers to remain steady as she punched in the numbers.

One ring. Two rings. Three rings. Her courage failed and the tip of her finger almost ended the fifteen seconds of heart-pounding waiting when a deep, husky voice came through the speaker.

"Hello."

She swallowed hard, willing herself to find the courage to speak. "Hey, Daniel. It's Melodie."

"Damn, woman. Are you trying to kill me?" No niceties. No apologies. Just the usual directness and arrogance. *God, how I've missed that.*

"Even if I had been, you would've killed me first. No note. No calls that evening. I was worried sick, Daniel." She'd wanted to think she was different, special. Part of her knew his reasoning for leaving in such a hurry was believable. The other allowed seeds of doubt and distrust from her youth to creep into her heart and make her believe she wasn't truly deserving of love. Fear of rejection not only served as the bookends of her life, it filled many chapters.

"Wait! What do you mean no note? I left you a note."

He had to be joking. "Where did you leave it? I looked and didn't find any."

"I jotted it on a piece of paper from your grocery list pad. It was the first thing I saw after getting the call. I put it on top of your mail pile, assuming you'd see it when you got home. Granted it wasn't a detailed note, but it was there. I swear it, Mel."

She hurried into the kitchen and started moving the stacks of mail around to look for the note. In the process, one of the unopened envelopes slipped off the counter and fell into the recycling bin just below. When she leaned over to pick it up, the corner of the patterned notepaper she used for her grocery list was sticking out from under another envelope. Tears sprang to her eyes. "I just found it. Must've fallen off the top of the stack and into the recycling bin."

She heard his exhale through the phone. "I know it wasn't much of a note, and I'm sorry I didn't get to call sooner, but once I landed I went straight to the hospital to check on Annie. When you didn't call after getting the note, I figured you were really pissed at me for leaving. Then you didn't answer your phone, and I had to explain over a voicemail. I swear to you, only my daughter needing me would make me break my promise to you."

"After my initial reaction, I spent a lot of time at the arboretum. I love being in nature. It calms me and helps me focus. Unfortunately, for people trying to call, cell service is sketchy at best. Considering our brief history on this subject, I didn't know what to think. What a mess we made of this."

"It is a mess, but we can fix it. You have to believe me. The only other woman who means anything to me right now is eight years old and loves Disney movies, especially *Beauty and the Beast*. I'd rather star as your Prince Charming or some other less hairy creature."

She wanted to keep the conversation on neutral ground. They'd made up, but it was too soon to return to the dangerous emotional territory of relationship talk. Those discussions always seemed to land them both in trouble. Time to turn the attention back to his daughter before this escalated any further and she either said something stupid or confessed she was falling in love.

Neither was a viable option at the moment. "Tell me more about what happened to Annie?"

"She and her mother were in a car accident." The tone of his voice was missing the normal confidence and cockiness she'd come to expect.

"Are they alright? How badly is Annie hurt?" Pseudo parenting kicked in. She may not be a mother, but she was a kick ass aunt.

"She's bruised and pretty sore but otherwise hanging in there."

Leaning heavily against the wall, she let out another breath. "I'm glad. And her mother?"

No response.

"Daniel? How's Annie's mom?"

"Fine." One word, terse and vague.

"Okay… Is Annie going home with her soon then?"

"No." One more word. Still terse. Still vague.

Melodie flopped onto the couch, unsure how to continue the conversation.

Thankfully, Daniel spoke. "I don't want to do this over the phone. I miss you and want to see you again."

Her heart fluttered with the possibilities his words conjured up. She thought she wouldn't see him again, at least not for the foreseeable future. "I miss you too."

Remembering her father's instructions about the makeup dinner on Friday, she asked. "Will your knight in shining armor suit fit in a carryon bag?" *He'd even look sexy in a suit of armor.*

"For you, I'm willing to check my bag to make sure it fits. Does milady need rescuing?"

She pulled one side of her bottom lip between her teeth. "Yes. In what I am promising will be my last act of rebellion, I didn't go to the party Saturday night. My actions put me squarely on top of my mother's personal hit list."

Daniel chuckled. "Did you say hit list or shit list?"

God, he was charming when he wanted to be. "One and the same with my mother."

"Well, I still have my nice new outfit."

"Well you can wear it Friday. I have to pay the piper."

"You have to what? Is that more of your book talk?"

Melodie couldn't help but laugh. "No. Just an expression meaning my presence is required at a family dinner on Friday night."

"Then let us accompany you."

"What?"

"I want to make it up to you and..."

The pause in his sentence was long enough to make her heart skip a beat or two. He'd said "us." Could that mean what she thought it did? "And?"

"I want you to meet Annie."

He wants me to meet his daughter? At least a hundred reasons why this wasn't a good idea flashed across her mind. Meeting his daughter equaled a new level of serious. She wanted to take this step with him, wanted to see him...touch him...kiss him. But this wasn't just about what she and Daniel wanted right now. She had to consider how Annie would react if things didn't work out between them. *I want them to work out!* "I'm not sure bringing Annie here is a good idea. We haven't known each other very long, and the time we have known each other has been a roller coaster of ups and downs."

His deep voice reached through the phone line and caressed her as though he were standing right in front of her. "That's what your mind says. What does your heart say?"

She paused for several moments before answering as she searched her heart for an honest answer. "My heart is scared."

"Of?"

"Being hurt again. Every time I open up and let someone in, I'm left with a new gaping hole when they leave. I'm not sure how much more I have to give."

"That's bullshit."

The bullet of accusation slammed solidly into her chest, making her physically recoil and almost drop the phone. "I'm sorry. What did you say?" Her mind quickly performed a currency exchange—sadness for anger.

"I said that's bullshit. You've hidden behind your jealousy of your sister and the pages of those damn books, wanting to believe life is supposed to be some fairy tale. Well, the books are called fiction for a reason, as you reminded me, and my guess is your sister's life is far from happily ever after.

Some people hide it better than others." His voice softened. "Besides, you just need to meet the right guy."

The words stung, but they also held some truth. She'd spent so long trying to live up to the image of her sister, she held every man she dated up to some imaginary standard. His issue with her and the books...well, they'd deal with that later. He didn't know women nearly as well as he thought if he didn't understand the concept of escapism. Books offered a retreat from the realities of life. "And you're the right guy?"

"I want to believe that, more than I've wanted to believe anything else in a long time. I know you're the only woman who went straight for my heart rather than my wallet."

"That's what you're basing all this on?" She wanted to believe him, wanted to experience all that life and love had to offer.

He laughed. "Hell no, but it's a good place to start. Bottom line, I want to see you again, and I can't leave Annie. Her mother can't take care of her right now. Come on, Mel. Say yes. You know we have something here. All the ups and downs are out of the way. Time for some smooth sailing, right?"

"Not going to argue with you on that point." Damn it all, this argument reminded her of fighting a losing battle. Despite every fear and the potential heartache this could cause, she knew agreement to this madness rested only one breath away.

"Think about how much fun it'll be to show up to dinner with a hot guy and a beautiful little girl. Your mom will be speechless."

Melodie allowed herself a moment to imagine the looks on the entire family's faces as she walked into the room with Daniel and Annie in tow. The image brought her a small measure of joy. "You have a point, though I've never known Mother to be speechless."

"First time for everything."

She exhaled loudly. "Alright, you win...again. When can I expect you?"

"Give me until tomorrow to make the arrangements, and then I'll text you the details."

"Okay. Daniel?"

"Yeah."

He may be a charmer, but even her heart had limits. "If you don't show this time, lose my number."

CHAPTER THIRTY-ONE

———

Thursday evening

"Are we there yet?"

Daniel smiled at his daughter's repeated question. She'd asked the same question from the moment the plane lifted off the tarmac in Mississippi. "We're here, baby. You remember what we talked about?"

He put the car in park and turned to the backseat and his daughter's angelic face, currently rolling her eyes at him.

"Yes, Daddy. Miss Melodie is a friend we're staying with. I'm to be polite and courteous and remember my manners." She put delicate little hands on her thin hips. "I am a lady, you know."

His chin lifted as his chest puffed up a bit. He still couldn't believe he'd been a part of creating something so amazing. "That you are, ma'am. Now, unfasten the seat belt, and don't forget your backpack."

"I know."

He laughed. Apparently turning eight made one all-knowing as Annie reminded him each time he gave her instructions. "How could I forget? You know everything."

She sighed heavily and fixed him with a "how silly can you be" look. "Duh, I'm eight now."

Like that explained it all. Too bad all the other problems in life couldn't be explained away that easily.

Grabbing the suitcase and the stuffed bear he'd given her at the hospital, which she assured him she simply couldn't go on a trip without as they were BFFs, he closed the trunk and took her hand. "You ready for this, kiddo?"

"What if she doesn't like me?" The emotion in her voice tore at his heart. He understood how she felt. The same annoying voice that plagued him about the accident kept whispering to him that he didn't deserve to love and be loved. *Yup, I'm losing it. They lock up people who hear voices.*

He may not deserve the kind of love he was after, but Annie sure as hell did. He paused and crouched down to eye level. "Remember me telling you Miss Melodie was a librarian?"

"Mmm hmm." Blonde curls bounced in rhythm with the nodding of her head.

"I forgot to mention she's a children's librarian. She loves kids."

Annie's eyes lit up. "Do you think she'd read a story to me?"

"She might if you ask nicely."

Confidence replaced the uncertainty. "I can do that."

Daniel returned his grip to her hand and began the longest walk of his life. He knew Melodie would love Annie, but asking her to consider a future with him and his "plus one" might be too much. His first priority needed to be his daughter since her mother wasn't going to be ready to assume parental responsibilities anytime soon…if ever.

Why were his nerves on edge more in this moment than during any battle he'd ever fought? *Before it was only my life, now it's my heart…and possibly Annie's as well.* Swallowing the fear, he knocked on the door, determined to not second-guess his decision to introduce the two most important women in his life to each other.

The tension fled, and his heart rate slowed the moment his jean-clad, green-eyed angel appeared in his line of sight. "Hey, Mel."

Her wary smile hinted enough warmth to give him hope. "Hey, yourself." Her attention ventured lower as she squatted down to Annie's eye level. "You must be Anastasia. May I call you Annie?"

A surge of pride and joy along with a hint of amusement filled his veins as the young girl curtsied.

"Pleasure to meet you, Miss Melodie. Please call me Annie."

The wary smile brightened as she took Annie's hand.

"Well, Annie please call me Melodie or Mel if you like."

Annie's gaze turned toward his to silently ask permission. Belle's family operated strictly under proper Southern rules of etiquette. All children referred to adults as Mr. or Miss. He nodded. "If it's okay with her, it's okay with me."

"Are you hungry, Annie? I happen to have the very best Chicago-style pizza joint on speed dial on my phone. You like pizza?"

"Yes, ma'am."

"Daniel, why don't you get your things settled, and I'll get dinner started."

He couldn't stand not touching her for one more moment. Closing the distance, his lips found the sweet spot right behind her ear. Though he preferred to kiss her senseless, he didn't want to explain his relationship with Mel to Annie until the dust settled, and all their cards were on the table. Belle had her faults, but Annie loved her, and he respected their relationship. "Thanks, Mel." He whispered, "I promise to explain everything after Annie goes to sleep."

She nodded but directed her next sentence to Annie. "Can you cook? I'm a horrible cook. Your dad probably already told you that though."

Her adorable little nose scrunched up. "I'm only eight." Again, as if that explained everything. "Daddy said you were a nice lady who might read me a story if I asked nicely."

"Well, he's right. As a matter of fact, if you check the dresser in my bedroom, there's a stack of books I brought home from the library I thought you might enjoy."

"Yay!!" Annie took off toward the back of the condo as though she knew exactly where the treasures were hidden.

Daniel started to call her back when Melodie's voice interrupted him. "Let her go. Nothing back there to hurt her. I even made the bed."

He moved in closer, pulling her body flush with his. He'd missed those soft curves. "Any chance we can unmake it in grand fashion later after Annie goes to bed?"

"I want to, but we probably need to talk first."

Possibly the most dreaded phrase any man could hear from a woman with whom he wanted to pursue a long-term relationship. So much he wanted to say...needed to say. He opted for the safe route for now. "Later, I promise. We'll talk." He shot a glance toward the bedroom. "Could I at least have a welcome back kiss?"

She returned his earlier gesture with a quick peck on his cheek.

"Not really the level of heat I was looking for." He buried his face in the sweet smelling curve of her neck.

She melted against him...just for a moment before her body stiffened. "I don't think it's a good idea. Annie could come down the hall any second."

So close.

He pulled out a chair and ran his fingers through the growing strands. A haircut needed to be on the to-do list. "Yeah, you're right, but damn I've missed you. I didn't have time to think about how much before. When Annie's grandfather called, I couldn't think of anything, or anyone, else. I called the airlines, booked a flight requiring a huge chunk of my miles, and left. All they'd tell me was she'd been in an accident." He took her hand and pulled her close. "Until you experience something like that, you can't imagine how it feels."

* * *

She embraced him and kissed him softly on the cheek before returning to the task of setting the table. "I'm pretty sure I do. Maybe not with a child, but I experienced it for a loved one after I received a bad-news phone call."

Daniel audibly sighed. Tom. Someone obviously called her with the bad news after his death. "Shit. You're right. I didn't mean anything by what I said, just sharing." He smiled. "I thought women liked that."

Forks and napkins followed. "We do, but I think we've established you've still got a lot to learn about women. And, I'm sure I have a lot to learn about men. I do know we both experience similar feelings of neglect, and we're easily convinced that we aren't worthy of love."

His head dropped. "I know I felt that when you walked out of the hotel room in Texas."

His words punched her squarely in the gut. The knock on the door stalled their conversation and gave her time to think. "Grab Annie, and I'll get the pizza."

He caught her arm before she walked away. "I never want to experience that again, and I never want you to either."

Finally, something they could agree on.

CHAPTER THIRTY-TWO

"Are you enjoying the extra cheese, Annie?" Melodie smiled at the melted strands dangling precariously between the young girl's mouth and the rest of her slice of pizza.

"Mmmm, very cheesy." She bit off the strands and giggled as the freed cheese wound around her hand.

"You could use a fork." Daniel groused.

Melodie used hers to free Annie's hand from its mozzarella prison. "No fun doing it that way, Dad. Lighten up."

Annie didn't respond as her mouth was full of deep-dish goodness, but her eyes sparkled as she nodded and grinned around the bite.

"I can see I'm outnumbered here. At least use a napkin to clean up the mess." He handed her a paper towel. "You need something bigger than a napkin tonight."

Her mouth finally empty, Annie grabbed the napkin and wiped her mouth. "I know." She turned her attention back to Melodie. "After pizza, will you read me some stories?"

Melodie's heart softened even further at the eager innocence sitting before her. "Of course. We'll have a princess pajama party once you're finished and have your bath." She cut a glance at Daniel to gauge his reaction. She was sure he'd been planning an adult pajama party for them…minus the pajamas.

"I can have a jamma party with Miss Melodie, can't I? Puhleese…"

Daniel's look said it all. He didn't want to agree but didn't stand any chance against the full measure of his daughter's exuberance. "Sure, princess. Now finish up, and I'll run your bath."

"Can Miss Melodie run my bath tonight?" Annie attacked the remaining bites of her pizza.

Daniel glanced in her direction. "If it's okay with Mel, it's okay with me."

"One bath coming up followed by a story or two."

Annie wiped her mouth and scurried off to get her pajamas.

"You and I are going to have an adult pajama party after the princess is asleep. This knight is going to get grumpy if he doesn't get to spend quality time with you soon."

Melodie stood and wrapped up the remaining pieces of pizza. "You need to brush up on your fairy tales. The knight only gets the girl after he slays the proverbial dragon."

He edged closer to her, the now familiar scent of his cologne washing over her like a powerful, yet evil, spell designed to make her forget her name. The softness of his lips, even warmer from the residual heat of the pizza, whispered across her mouth. A phantom touch similar to their earliest kisses and still capable of rendering her weak in the knees. If she didn't find the strength to pull away soon, she'd miss yet another party, a princess pajama party, no less.

His question came out in pieces as he nibbled gently on her ear. "And...who...or what...is the dragon...to win...the hand... of milady?"

"Miss Melodie!" The impatient voice called out from the bathroom. "I'm ready for my bath."

"Coming, Annie." The spell broken, she remembered where she'd been heading in her conversation with Daniel before he turned his charms on her. She kissed him fully on the lips before heading toward the bathroom. "My mother."

"What?"

"You want to capture milady's heart? Slay my biggest dragon, Marie Alexander."

* * *

Her mother? Great. His very first family function since the divorce, and he had the task of dealing with her mother. Daniel finished clearing away the remnants of dinner before pulling out his laptop. The giggling coming from the back of the apartment indicated all was well with his daughter. He'd check in on both of them in a little bit, but first it was time to put all those skills he'd learned in the army for getting at the truth to good use.

The lack of noise from the rest of the house finally registered. How long had he been pouring through different search engines to learn about the two other Alexander women? Ten o'clock. Hours past Annie's bedtime and time to finish the adult conversation from earlier. The sooner they dealt with all of this, the better.

He walked quietly to the bedroom. His heart melted at the small splash of blonde and the larger splash of chocolate brown hair spread in beautiful disarray over the pillows. The angelic faces captured perfectly in sleep. A fairy tale book lay open between them, and their matching pink tops completed the feminine picture. Leaning over, he placed a tender kiss on each of their foreheads, removed the book, and tucked them in. As he went to turn out the light, he noticed an old family picture. Without a doubt, Evelyn resembled her mother, not only in personality, as Melodie had shared with him, but also in looks. Her father had the same dark hair and kind eyes as his sleeping beauty.

He turned off the light. The picture of a younger Evelyn Alexander sparked recognition and an idea. This time he wouldn't let Melodie down. He knew exactly how to slay this dragon, and a few phone calls or texts to some old friends would give him the weapon to ensure she didn't have to fear her dragon anymore.

Friday

"Are you divas, I mean ladies, about ready? We don't want to be late." Daniel had no idea why it took women, especially one eight years old, so long to get ready. He and Annie had spent most of the day shopping for a new dress, along with all the accessories Melodie insisted Annie needed. One thing was certain. If he convinced Melodie to marry him someday, without a doubt, he'd be outnumbered, outmaneuvered, and outvoted on every decision in which she and Annie collaborated. Between the sweet smile of his daughter and the smoldering eyes of his lover, he didn't stand a chance.

Beautiful. Not a fancy word, but the only one that came to mind when they finally emerged from the bathroom. Annie's powder blue dress, complete with ruffles and lace, made her look exactly like a fairy princess. White gloves and the matching purse completed her outfit. Damn, he'd done good. He and Belle might not have done anything else good together, but Annie represented the best in both of them. *I want to believe I deserve such beauty in my life.*

His eyes shifted to Melodie, and the warmth he'd experienced in his heart from his daughter surged lower and created an entirely different response as he drank in the sight of the woman he'd fallen head over heels in love with. The dark blue of her dress accented every asset she possessed. The curves…curves he'd missed holding, seemed to call out to him from behind their protective barriers, begging for his touch. The waves he'd loved running his fingers through swept up in some elaborate hairdo that left an appropriate amount of strands to cover the soft curve of her neck. Another curve he intended on spending time reacquainting himself with later.

A tug on his sport coat brought him out of the fantasy. "Daddy, don't we look pretty?"

He crouched down and brushed a lock of gold from Annie's cheek. "No, princess, you both look beautiful. So beautiful, in fact, you made your prince speechless."

Her laughter broke the spell. "You're so silly. Let's go. I'm ready for the party."

"Grab your coat, and I'll help Mel with hers." He picked up the lightweight coat and slid it over her slender arms, his lips finding their way to the most recent curve he'd been admiring. "Beautiful. Sexy. I have all kinds of adjectives to share with you."

She turned in his arms and returned the kiss, chaste, but at least the softness found his lips this time. "Thank you. Are you sure you're ready for this?"

He couldn't help himself. He pulled her into a hug and, for a moment, enjoyed the yielding feel of her body cushioned against his. This couldn't be more right, and now that he'd found her, he harbored zero plans to ever let her go. She shivered slightly in his embrace as he whispered in her ear, "I've never been more ready for anything in my life."

CHAPTER THIRTY-THREE

———

The familiar knot of dread settled low in her stomach as they pulled into the drive. The two-story, brick home provided an imposing picture of elegance and affluence to anyone who passed by. To her, a keen sense of dread and a lifetime of never quite being good enough. A warm hand on her thigh dispelled the spreading chill. *Breathe.* This was her family, not a firing squad. She allowed herself a small smile. Sometimes dinner conversation was worse than a firing squad.

"We've got this, Mel." He put the car in park and turned to the backseat. "We'll watch out for her, won't we?"

"I know, Daddy. We always protect the fair maidens in the kingdom along with the king and queen. 'Cept for when they're wicked. You're not wicked, are you, Mel?"

Their efforts worked, and she released some of the tension with a bright smile. *Only when I'm in bed with your daddy.* "I try very hard not to be. Shall we go inside the castle?"

Annie took her hand and stared up at her with wide blue eyes. "There isn't a wicked queen inside the house is there?"

Melodie crouched down next to her and offered a reassuring smile. "Not wicked but sometimes she gets a little grumpy, especially at me. Don't worry though. I promise your Dad and I won't let her be grumpy with you. Okay to go in now?"

"Yes." Her heart warmed at Annie's confident reply. Maybe this dinner would be different.

Melodie knocked on the door. Her father's smiling face greeted her. "Mel, glad you could make it." He pulled her into a hug and whispered, "And on time too. That should help."

"Melodie, is that you?" Her mother's voice rang out from somewhere within the house.

"Yes, Mother, we're here." She stepped into the house with her entourage close behind.

A moment later, the commanding presence of Marie Alexander filled the room. "So good of you to actually show up this time."

Daniel's deep voice prevented her from responding. "That was my fault, ma'am." He guided Annie to his side. "Actually, our fault."

"And you are?"

"Mother, this is Daniel Bresland and his daughter, Anastasia…Annie."

Annie curtsied. "Pleasure to meet you, ma'am."

Was that the tiniest of cracks in her mother's tough exterior as her gaze fell onto Annie? Evelyn's two-point-three children provided grandsons, but thus far no granddaughters had been gifted.

Marie crouched down to be closer to eye level with Annie. "And why is it you were responsible for my daughter not showing up to the last party we hosted?"

"She was in a car wreck with her mother, my ex-wife. I'm sure as a parent you can understand why I needed to leave in a hurry to make certain my princess was safe."

The challenge in Daniel's voice didn't go unnoticed by Marie, and she stood to her full five-foot-ten inches to return her attention to him. "That explains why you weren't here, not why she wasn't."

Here it comes. She wasn't even home five minutes, and her mother was ready to serve up the main course with her head on a silver platter. She opened her mouth to respond again, the knot in her stomach expanding and growing in density with each passing moment.

Daniel's arm slid around her waist as he pulled her close, quelling the rising panic. "As I explained, my fault. In my distress, I left in a hurry. Unfortunately, the note, explaining my absence, fell off the counter, so she didn't see it. Mel was worried for my safety and so upset she lost track of the time trying to reach me. You remember what it's like to be so into another person you forget about everyone and everything else, don't you?" He finished his statement by pulling Melodie closer and kissing her tenderly on the cheek. "From the moment I met your daughter, there's been an undeniable attraction—something special I can't explain. Of course, now that I've met her mother, there's no question where she gets her breathtaking beauty from."

Oh, he was good...very good.

Daniel released Annie's hand long enough to focus his attention solely on Melodie. His fingers caressed her cheek before lifting her chin for a tender kiss—not the one they'd both been wanting since he arrived yesterday, but enough. The undeniable pull of attraction—need—maybe even love—filled her body. Of their own freewill, her hands slid up his chest and around his neck, savoring the moment. Before they could get too swept away in the moment, he broke their connection.

His eyes never left hers. "Surely, Mrs. Alexander, you can understand, and forgive her—forgive us—for missing the party. Melodie's shared with me how successful her big sister is. I'm sure there'll be more occasions to celebrate."

Another knock on the door saved Marie from answering. Her face brightened considerably. "That must be Evelyn and her family."

Daniel didn't miss a beat. "I'm really looking forward to meeting her. I think we may have actually met before."

What the...? After all the conversations they'd had about her sister. Not once did he mention he'd met her. Familiar feelings of jealousy settled like rocks in her stomach. If he even flirted with her sister...She moved aside to allow her mother to pass, not missing the curious look Marie sent Daniel at his statement. Anyone who knew Evelyn was of interest to her. "You never told me you knew Ev?"

"I realized it last night, but as I recall, you had a princess pajama party, and I ended up spending the night on the couch."

She blushed, both embarrassed at the direction of her thoughts and relieved she'd fallen asleep reading to Annie. The woman in her knew she wouldn't have been able to resist Daniel's charms if they'd been alone, and especially not if his tempting body was next to hers in bed. "Are you going to tell me now?"

He kissed her again, pushing curiosity to a dark corner of her mind. If he kept this up, they'd be in major trouble with her mother when she dragged Daniel to her old bedroom and had her way with him.

His whispered breath across her ear turned her knees to jelly. "I'll fill you in later when you're naked and in my arms. Until then, know I intend to slay both dragons in your life tonight with one fell swoop of my sword."

"Eeewww, gross!" Her youngest nephew's protest at the public display of affection prevented her from saying or doing anything more.

She turned from Daniel's embrace and scooped Jason into her arms, tickling as she held him close. "Gross? Gross! I'm sure your mommy and daddy kiss too."

His laughter filled the air as he squealed. "Stop, Auntie Mel. Stop!"

"Jason, not so loud. You know how Gramma Marie doesn't like loud noises." Evelyn's chilly voice robbed the room of warmth.

Melodie rolled her eyes and then winked at Jason before setting him down. "We'll wait until later to get into trouble. It's too early to make both Mom and Gramma mad at us."

He sighed. "Okay, Auntie Mel."

"I brought someone for you to play with tonight though. Would you like to meet her?"

"You brought a girl?" His nose wrinkled.

"I'm a lady, not a girl." The indignant voice of an offended eight year old filled the space around her.

Melodie turned him around. "Jason, meet Annie. Annie, this is Jason. He's seven."

His green eyes gave her the once-over, apparently deciding whether she'd make a worthy playmate. "Do you like to play castles and dragons?"

"Can I be a princess?"

He shrugged his shoulders. "Sure, why not. Mom, can we go play before dinner?"

"Ask properly."

Melodie fought the urge to roll her eyes again. If her nephews turned out not to have anger or mommy issues, it'd be a miracle. Like she had room to talk. She was going to make changes in this part of her life as well...just not tonight.

"May..." he stretched the word out for effect, "we go play before dinner, please?"

She nodded and smiled proudly. "Yes, you may."

Jason took Annie by the hand, and they ran off to play.

"Young love. How sweet," Melodie offered to the now-quiet room of adults. Evelyn's husband and her oldest nephew were absent. "Where's the rest of the family?"

"Swim meet."

Melodie didn't even ask why Evelyn didn't attend. If mother requested her presence, she'd ignore everyone and everything else to accommodate her wishes.

Before she could say or ask anything else, Marie interjected. "Melodie, why don't you help me in the kitchen? You and I have some things to talk about. Evelyn, please entertain her guest. His name is Daniel, and he professes to be 'so into her.' I'm sure you have questions for him."

The sinking feeling in Melodie's heart compared to the *Titanic* and her newfound love story as tragic as the one in the movie. By the time Ev was done grilling him, she'd be lucky if he didn't rescue Annie from the playroom and disappear again before dinner was served. Thanks to her mother, she wouldn't even be here to help him. At least with her big sister being happily married, she hoped she didn't have to worry about Ev trying to steal her man this time. *My man... like the sound of that.*

She grabbed his hand and gave him a kiss on the cheek. "Good luck. Never let her see you sweat."

He pulled her closer and kissed the curve of her neck, unearthing another secret—the location of her sweet spot. "I've got this, Mel. One slayed dragon coming up." He winked and pushed her off toward the kitchen and her own personal firing squad.

"Dad, you coming to the kitchen to help?"

He winked and smiled but shook his head. "Nope. I'm going to play with the kids. Safest place in the house right now, I think."

CHAPTER THIRTY-FOUR

———

"How did you meet my sister, and what exactly do you want from her?" Evelyn's tone reminded him of being cross-examined by Belle's attorney during their divorce proceedings.

He gestured toward the couch in the formal sitting room just off the foyer. "Would you like to sit down before we begin?"

"I prefer to stand." Evelyn crossed her arms and leveled a glare in his direction. "Now, answer my questions."

If that's how she wanted to play, fine. "I'll answer your questions, and then you answer mine."

Her blue eyes blazed, but she nodded. Melodie hadn't exaggerated the focus of the elder Alexander women. "Mel and I met in Dallas…well, on the plane between Chicago and Dallas." He smiled, remembering their first encounter.

"Melodie hates to fly, and I'm supposed to believe she fell head over heels for you in the two hours or so it takes to get to Dallas?"

If every other man Melodie brought home received this treatment, no wonder she guarded her heart so carefully. *Or maybe she hasn't brought too many other men home.* "You obviously aren't a hopeless romantic like your sister. It was love almost at first sight for me when I met her on the flight. She took a little more convincing."

"You seduced my sister." An accusation rather than a question clearly delivered in her tone.

"Damn straight I did. She's worth the effort, emotion, and energy it takes to get through the walls she's built around her heart, thanks to growing up in your shadow." Face the enemy head-on. No subversion. No strategy. Time to set up the kill.

"My sister's inability to find a man is *my* fault?"

Anger replaced accusation in her tone. Daniel knew his target now rested clearly in his sites, an eminent strike. "Not entirely. Your mother played a pretty significant role, from what I've been able to learn in the time I've known your sister. Marie compares Melodie to you in everything."

Her shoulders straightened. "I may set the bar high, but I'm very successful. Melodie would do well to be like me."

Time for the kill. He stepped closer, meeting her challenge and lowering his voice so no one else could hear. "So she should cheat on her husband when she's in India on business with a soldier who's on leave?"

Evelyn's red cheeks drained of color, and the fury in her eyes morphed from surprise to recognition and, finally, embarrassment. "How could you…? I mean… It was…"

Daniel wished Mel could witness the crack in her sister's façade, but that wasn't part of the plan. Family was important to him, and he wanted to see these fences mended, not torn down completely. "The world is a small place. When I saw a family picture, a candid shot, rather than the head shot from your firm, I remembered seeing you with my buddy when we were on leave. I never forget a face. You didn't even take off your wedding ring. Tsk, tsk. What would your family say? What would Marie say if she knew her perfect daughter happened to be flawed and human like the rest of us?"

"You wouldn't!" Both a question and a demand.

"By the way, you broke my buddy's heart. In case you care. I'm not going to tell Melodie because there's something I want more than airing your dirty little secret."

"I'm listening."

The sword raised, ready to hand off to Evelyn to finish slaying the real dragon, Marie. "Two things. First, stop treating your sister like she's a second-class citizen, and see her for the amazing woman she is, even if that happens to be different from you and your mother. Second, find a way to get your mother to back off as well."

She shook her head. "Number one I can do. Mother has a mind of her own and is very set in her ways."

He shrugged. "Your problem, not mine. You're the brilliant and highly successful attorney. Make it happen, or I'll let

Mom in on our little secret, and you can deal with the fallout of your little indiscretion."

Evelyn's eyes cleared, and the thin line of her mouth hardened. The ice in her blue eyes fired in Daniel's direction. "I'm going to find out your secrets and tell Melodie. Everyone has secrets."

Sibling rivalry he could deal with, especially since he had nothing left to hide. "I'm an open and easy-to-read book, so give it your best shot. Besides, I've already confessed all my secrets to your sister. Surprise, surprise, she still wants me in her life, in her bed, and in her heart. Apparently she's more willing to overlook flaws than you and your mother."

"You're a bastard."

Daniel smiled, thinking of all the times Melodie had inferred the very same characterization through things she said or did. She was classier than her sister, though, and had never called him one straight out. *Dr. Jekyll and Mr. Hyde are her favorite nicknames for me.* "This is no secret to your sister either. I'm a bastard. You're a bitch. Enough name-calling. We both know who we are. The question is, are we going to partner up to make life easier for your sister, or am I about to make your life more difficult?"

The redness covering her face and her clenched fists might intimidate others, but he stood his ground. He had her right where he wanted her—she'd protect her secret.

She moved into his personal space and extended her hand. "Partners."

CHAPTER THIRTY-FIVE

Daniel and Evelyn entered the formal dining room. Melodie's mother and father took their places at each end of the table while Evelyn and Jason occupied the side opposite of Melodie and her "family."

"Dinner smells wonderful." Daniel offered, placing a quick kiss on Melodie's cheek before sitting on the end next to her mother.

"Chicken parmesan, one of mother's specialties." Melodie desperately tried to read the look on either Daniel or her sister's faces, but both remained passive and in control as far as she could tell. If her sister had turned Daniel against her...

Marie's voice cut in as she started the plates of food around the table. "You must know by now Melodie's idea of cooking a nice dinner is speed-dialing a restaurant other than the local pizza joint."

And so it starts. She didn't even have food on her plate, and the picking had started.

Daniel interjected, "Fortunately for us then, I'm not interested in Mel for her cooking ability. I'm no Emeril either, and after the MREs and army cooking for several years, I've learned to be grateful for whatever is placed in front of me." He leaned forward and winked in Melodie's direction. "Besides, I think taking a cooking class together would be fun. What do you think?"

The thought of either Daniel or her taking a cooking class required her to suppress a bubble of laughter, but playing along with his game might be fun. Of course Evelyn would side with Mother, but maybe it was time for a good fight. "I think that's a wonderful idea. I'll do some research and find some classes for us."

Marie rolled her eyes. "There she goes again. If she spent more time actually doing something rather than researching it, she'd be as successful as her sister rather than dallying around putting books away all day."

First my cooking, now my job. She's not wasting any time tonight.

Evelyn chimed in, "Mother, please. Let's enjoy the wonderful meal you've prepared while you tell us about your upcoming trip to China."

Did her big sister just defend her? She couldn't remember the last time Evelyn intervened, especially not in front of guests.

The delay tactic worked, and for the next several minutes, Marie expounded about her latest clients, their importance, and the planned trip to China.

"Mulan is from China," Annie shared once Marie finished.

"Mulan?" The older woman smiled in her direction.

"The hero..." Annie looked to Melodie for confirmation. Receiving a nod, she continued, "The heroine in the story Melodie read me last night."

"Melodie certainly enjoys burying herself in a book, even if she forgets a real world exists outside of the pages."

Well, the break was nice while it lasted.

"She's the best story reader ever." Annie returned to her meal.

"Thank you, Annie." With each word of praise or reassurance from the wonderful people sitting on either side of her, her confidence ventured the smallest of steps away from a lifetime of anxiety and inferiority.

Jason added, "You're right, princess, Auntie Mel's stories are better than anyone else's. Everyone at the library loves when she reads during story time."

Evelyn turned her attention to her son. "Princess?"

Jason's expression turned earnest, his eyes focused solely on his mother. "She's a princess, and I'm her brave knight, like in the stories you used to read me. Remember, Mommy?"

Her big sister's expression softened and revealed the slightest hint of regret. Her perfectly manicured nails tousled his hair. "I remember. I guess it's been a while, hasn't it?"

He nodded. "Mmm hmm."

"Maybe I can read you one tonight when we get home?"

Melodie blinked a couple times. Whatever Daniel had said to Evelyn certainly had prompted a slight and positive change in her actions...*like he's done for me.*

Jason's eyes brightened. "That would be awesome! But..." he chewed on his bottom lip.

"Oh, for heaven's sake, what is it Jason?" Marie's fork hit the plate with a loud scrape, drawing everyone's attention her way.

"Mother, please." Melodie's heart constricted at the tears forming in her nephew's eyes.

Evelyn turned her attention away from Marie's and spoke to her son. "It's always important to mean what you say and say what you mean. You should never be afraid to voice your thoughts or opinions."

Not waiting for Jason to answer, Marie continued. "I agree completely, Evelyn. There are people who make things happen in life and others who read about it." Her attention diverted to Daniel. "Don't you agree? You want your daughter to be a leader in life, don't you?"

Daniel smiled at Annie. "I want the very best for her, everything the world has to offer. I served my country in an effort to make sure she had the freedom to pursue whatever her heart desires." He turned his attention completely to Marie. "What I want most for her, though, is to be happy. So wherever her path to happiness takes her, is good enough for me."

Melodie blinked quickly to keep the tears at bay. Daniel's words echoed the sentiment she'd wanted to hear from her mother for years. She wanted to be good enough. Turning to Daniel, she reached out and squeezed his hand. "Beautifully said."

Marie interjected. "Yes, I do suppose you'd feel that way Melodie. Your father certainly ascribed to that sentiment with you. Didn't you, dear?"

"Marie." Her father's quiet voice cut through the escalating tension and sarcasm. "Perhaps we should move on to other subjects for the dinner discussion?"

Melodie's attention split between her mother and father. *Now is not the time for a family fight.* "Great idea, Dad. Evelyn, how is Michael doing this year in swim?"

Marie interjected and smiled broadly at Evelyn. "Before you do, dear, why don't you fill Melodie in on all the news she missed at the party we hosted for you last week? It really was quite an accomplishment."

Melodie noticed her sister shoot Daniel a quick glance before taking a bite of her food. *What the hell? I've never seen Ev like this.* When she finished her bite, she shrugged her shoulders. "I was lucky enough to settle a big deal in favor of one of our clients."

"Earned your firm millions." Marie beamed with pride.

"That's great, Ev. I'm very proud of you." Melodie really was proud of her big sister.

Evelyn nodded. "Thank you. About Michael, he's really improved on his lap times."

"Yes, darling, that's wonderful. Do tell us more about your deal, though. You know how I love the details. Maybe we could all learn something from your experience. I'm certain hearing about initiative and hard work would be a good life lesson."

"Or…" Steven interrupted, "we could hear more about Michael's lap times. I'd love to hear how my eldest grandson is doing."

Daniel turned, lowered his head, and grinned at Melodie. She was glad he found this exchange amusing. She was rather embarrassed by it all. Reaching under the table, she put her hand on his thigh and squeezed. Maybe for reassurance…maybe to keep him from grabbing Annie and running.

Marie stood. "Fine, you catch up on Michael, and I'll get dessert." She leveled intense blue eyes in the direction of her husband. "I'm sure we can discuss this more later."

With those words, she turned and left the room. At Marie's departure, Jason's eyes grew wide as moisture collected and spilled from his baby blues. "Is Gramma mad at me?"

Annie jumped out of her chair and ran to the other side of the table. She threw her arms around him. "It's okay, my brave knight." She leaned in, her voice lowered in a comforting tone. "The grumpy queen is gone."

Jason leaned into Annie's embrace, "Thank you, princess."

Steven smiled affectionately at the children. "Don't worry Jason—if Gramma is mad at anyone, it's me." He winked at Annie. "Any ideas on how I can handle the grumpy queen?"

Melodie smiled at her father and was relieved to see Daniel and Evelyn smile too. Daniel's hand covered hers, still resting on his thigh, the pride on his face was evident. Annie moved away from Jason to the elder Alexander male at the table and wrapped her small arms around his waist. "Maybe your queen needs you to slay a dragon for her. My daddy says that's what wins her heart."

He smiled and returned Annie's hug. "You might be right, princess. Maybe this old king needs to pull out his rusty ol' sword and go to battle." He looked to Daniel and Melodie. "I'm sorry if our dinner conversation has been uncomfortable for you and your daughter."

Daniel stood and extended his hand toward Annie to bring her back to her chair. "Don't worry, sir. I come from a family where it wouldn't be a real dinner if at least one person didn't storm away before the end of the meal."

"Regardless, you and Annie…"

"Princess," Annie interjected.

Steven winked. "You and the princess are our guests. I promise the next time you come over for dinner, things will be better."

Did her father say next time? Could she have finally found someone who wasn't intimidated by Evelyn and her mother and had Dad's approval too? *Too good to be true.*

As if on cue, Marie arrived with coffee and dessert. Melodie only half listened to the conversation, smiling and nodding at the appropriate times. *This feels so right.* Finally, dinner and dessert were over. A sense of peace, despite the ongoing tension, wrapped her in contentment—the same sensation as a warm fuzzy blanket on a cold winter night.

Annie stood and moved to stand in front of Marie. She executed the perfect Southern curtsy. "Everything was wonderful, Your Majesty. Thank you for dinner."

Steven smiled at Melodie and Daniel. "That's a beautiful princess you have there. Isn't she, Marie?"

A small smile replaced the usual hard lines of Marie's mouth. "She is rather charming." She nodded at Annie. "Now, why don't you let Jason show you to the coat room, and you two bring the coats back for Mel and your daddy?"

The little girl bounced with excitement. "We can do that, can't we, brave knight?"

Jason smiled and wiped at the tear stains on his cheek. He looked up at his mother, silently asking for permission. At her slight nod and smile, he jumped down from the table, grabbed Annie's hand, and they ran off.

Once they were out of the room, Marie turned toward them. "Daniel, a pleasure meeting you. Thank you for joining us for dinner. Melodie, I will expect you to not miss another family party. Now, if everyone will excuse me."

Children's laughter could be heard from the other room. Evelyn laughed. "I think he may be as into Annie as her daddy is into Mel."

Melodie couldn't believe her ears—Evelyn laughed. By far, the strangest dinner party she'd ever been to at her parent's house. She couldn't leave without saying anything. "Thanks for sticking up for me with Mom earlier, Ev. It means a lot."

Her older sister's blue eyes darkened for a moment and cut to Daniel before a loud bellow came from the back of the house. "Evelyn!"

Steven stood. "I'll go." He moved over to Melodie and gave her a hug. "Take your guests and go home. I'll check in with you later." He turned and extended his hand to Daniel. "Pleasure meeting you, son. Amazing little girl you have there— reminds me of Mel at that age."

"Thank you, sir. It was a pleasure meeting you and the rest of your family."

"Evelyn!"

"I feel bad leaving you two to deal with her."

Fatigue and stress she'd never noticed showed in her sister's eyes. A pang of compassion for her archrival throughout life flooded her limbs, weighting them with empathy. Maybe being the apple of Mother's eye carried different burdens, equally as challenging as being the black sheep of the family?

Jason and Annie appeared with the coats.

Evelyn secured the garments before they hit the floor and handed them to the adults. "Go. I'll see to Mother."

Warmth and a sense of comfort settled over Melodie as Daniel's hand came to rest on her lower back, guiding her toward the door. She kissed her father on the cheek and clasped Annie's hand as they made their way to the car. Once on the interstate, she looked over to the man whose presence in her life defied explanation. Equal parts arrogance and compassion, a combination she was slowly learning to appreciate. Though aggravating at times, his ways of dealing with people were proving effective. Maybe she could learn a thing or two from him. Researching Daniel at length possessed the possibility of endless rewards.

"When we get home, are you going to share how you tamed my sister?"

His eyes cut in her direction briefly before he shrugged and returned his attention to the road. "Let's just say you're better at hiding secrets than your sister."

Evelyn has a secret? "You blackmailed her?"

"I employed a tactical advantage to achieve our mutual goal. You wanted your sister off your back, and I needed to slay a couple of dragons tonight." His rugged jaw, barely visible in the glow of the dash lights, sported a shadow from the outgrowth of his beard, matching the do-what-you-have-to-do mentality he'd demonstrated since she met him. The hard set of his jaw softened, and a small smile appeared. "Did I prove my worth to milady tonight?"

"Daddy, I'm still hungry." Annie chimed in from the backseat. "A princess should never be hungry, right?"

Melodie smiled. "Well, we didn't get much dessert, did we? There's a place that has the best frozen yogurt. We can stop when we exit the interstate."

Daniel took her hand and squeezed. "I think some frozen yogurt sounds good. Let's eat some there, and then we'll grab extra for home. Once the princess is in bed, you and I are going to have the talk we've wanted to have since I arrived."

Looking out the window as the cars and buildings moved by her line of vision at a rapid pace, Melodie admitted to herself for the first time, in a very long time, the last thing she wanted to do was talk.

CHAPTER THIRTY-SIX

———

"This coffee fro-yo is amazing. I can't believe I've never had this flavor before." Daniel took another generous bite. A second later his face contorted in pain. *Damn!* He placed the heel of his hand against his eye socket. He should know better by now. A moment later a glass was placed in his hand.

"Here, sip some water, it will help. Those ice cream headaches are painful." Melodie's voice soothed the headache and his heart. Her family wasn't perfect. Hell, no one's was. But, he and Annie fit in nicely. He grinned behind the rim of the glass, not wanting Melodie to see. With a bit of persuasion, he might even be able to convince Evelyn not to hate him. *That might take a while...* Blackmail was never a good way to start a relationship, but a man's gotta do what a man's gotta do.

"Ewww, that's gross." Annie wrinkled her nose before taking another bite of her vanilla yogurt.

"Why don't you like anything but vanilla?" Melodie wiped her mouth and then kept her attention squarely on Annie. Once she had more time to accept the doctor's diagnosis, they'd talk about options if she wanted to have more children. But he hadn't lied. He could see himself content and happy with just Melodie and Annie as his family. *And what about the men who can never return to their families?*

"Vanilla is the best, just ask anyone."

He fought the urge to sigh—she sounded like her mother. Belle never appreciated the finer things in life—fried chicken, barbeque ribs, or even something besides vanilla ice cream. "You've never even tried anything but vanilla, little girl. How can you know you don't like anything else?"

"I know. When you have the best already, you don't have to try anymore." Annie delivered the lines in a singsong voice as though it were the most simple and logical statement in the world.

Out of the mouths of babes... He was still going to try to get his daughter to try something besides vanilla someday, but when it came to women he was pretty sure he'd just found the best. No need to keep looking. "You may have a point, but we'll talk more about this subject later. Finish up your boring vanilla. Then it's bath and bed time."

"Mel, will you read me a bedtime story?"

Daniel's heart surged as Melodie's fingers tousled through Annie's curls, her smile radiating a tenderness confirming that maybe, just maybe, she was the one for him.

"How about two since you were such a good girl tonight?"

"Yay! Thank you. May I be excused to get my bath?" Excitement danced in her blue eyes.

Daniel smiled at his daughter. She'd handled herself like a true lady tonight. "As long as your belly is full, you may be excused. Grab your pajamas, and I'll be there in a minute to start the water for you."

The moment the blonde head disappeared, he pulled Melodie's chair closer to him. "Do I get a bedtime story tonight?" He couldn't help himself. He nibbled on her ear, soliciting a small moan of pleasure from her very kissable lips. "The knight would like to claim his treasure for slaying the dragons."

His eyes closed as her lips, still cool from the frozen treats they'd been eating, smothered his, the pressure releasing his strong need for her—a need he barely kept in check from hour to hour. The tip of his tongue swept across her mouth, his coffee and her chocolate flavors mingling into something far better than vanilla could ever hope to be. The vibration from her hum of pleasure reverberated through his body, ratcheting his desire another level higher.

"Daddy, I'm ready!" The shout from the back of the apartment doused the flames of his desire with ice cold water.

"Be right there, princess." He brushed his thumb across her well-kissed lips. "Clothing is not required for my bedtime story, in case you were wondering." He couldn't stop touching her. There was something about her body that called to him like a siren song. "As a matter of fact, I've outlawed bedtime clothes in my kingdom."

"Oh? I thought only the king could make the laws in the kingdom." She guided his hand under her shirt. Her breast fit perfectly in the palm of his hand. *She's perfect.* Circling the tip with his thumb, excitement pulsed through his body as the nipple hardened under his touch. He longed to spend hours touching, tasting, and teasing just to hear her gasp with pleasure.

"The king rewarded me for bravery in battle and slaying not one, but two dragons."

His body tightened impossibly farther when her hand slid between his legs to gently stroke his arousal.

"Far be it from me to disappoint the king or his brave knight."

This woman represented a vixen, a tormentor, and salvation all wrapped into one. Before this night ended, he would not only have his bedtime story but would try to find the courage to tell her how much he cared for her. He wanted whatever this was—to never end.

"Daddy!"

"I won't be long. Make those bedtime stories for Annie short ones, okay?"

Her smile and the dark intensity of her eyes almost made him forget his daughter. "The shortest ones I can find."

One quick kiss and he left her to usher in the quickest bath in Annie's eight-year history.

CHAPTER THIRTY-SEVEN

———

Melodie indulged herself in gawking after Daniel's backside as he retreated from their all-too-brief make-out session to tend to Annie. Part of her was emotionally exhausted from the bizarre family dinner, the other part hummed with excitement at the thought of sharing Daniel's bed again.

Singing quietly to herself, she put away the leftovers. A small part of her brain vied for attention, wondering how the scenes were unfolding with her parents and Evelyn. Had it been cowardly of her to leave Evelyn to deal with mother alone? Would her father's patience with her mother finally wear thin? Melodie's old friend, guilt, stepped proudly into the spotlight of her emotions, relegating the happier feelings to the shadows.

A knock on the door stalled the downward spiral of her mood. She checked the peephole to see who'd be visiting at this late hour. The perfectly coiffed blonde hair could belong to only one person—Evelyn.

Melodie closed her eyes for a moment, summoning strength before opening the door. "Ev? What's wrong?"

Her sister stepped to the side, revealing the eager young face of her nephew. "Someone wanted a bedtime story and claimed severe disappointment his evening with the princess had ended." Her tired smile mirrored the exhausted sound of her voice. "And I wanted to talk to you."

"Come on in. You want some frozen yogurt? We brought extra home."

"No, thank you. Mother insisted on sending some food home with us, and Jason begged for McDonald's ice cream on the way over here. Crazy kid picked a vanilla cone. Personally, I would've gone for the hot fudge sundae."

Could this be the same sister she'd grown up with? The one who always followed the rules and never colored outside the lines. She looked at Jason. "You and the princess are destined to be best friends. She only likes vanilla too."

His toothy grin warmed her heart. She couldn't love him any more if he were her own. "Well, duh, vanilla is the best. Where's Annie?"

"She's getting her bath. Why don't you go back to my room and pick out one story for you and one for her, and then I'll read them both."

"Yay!" Jason tore off into the back room, and Melodie waited for her sister to yell at him for not asking permission, running in the house...something.

Nothing.

"Ev, are you alright? How's Mom?" For the second time that night, lines around her sister's eyes and the tension in her jaw displayed prominently on her otherwise perfect visage.

"Can we sit down?"

"Sure. Let me ask Daniel to look after the kids for a few minutes."

"He's a keeper. Don't let this one get away."

Melodie fought the urge to look outside to see if a full moon hung in the sky. Maybe body snatchers provided an explanation, or some type of weird paranormal occurrence. One of the strangest nights she could remember. Arriving at the bathroom, her heart melted. Daniel was brushing out Annie's hair. He was such a good dad. Another quick stab of pain flashed through her heart. He knew they could never have children, not in the traditional manner anyway, and he'd stood by and supported her. Her heart fluttered, warming her from the inside out. *Maybe this is what love feels like.*

"Mel, everything okay?" Daniel's intense gaze held her motionless for a moment. He had such beautiful eyes.

His voice snapped her out of her thoughts. "I think so. Jason and Evelyn are here."

"My knight?" Annie started bouncing. Did she and Jason have a hidden stash of sugar somewhere?

She grinned at Daniel. Those two were fast friends. "Yes, he's waiting for you in my room. Pick out some stories, and I'll be in after I talk to Jason's mommy, okay?"

Annie saddened a bit. "I miss my mommy."

Daniel pulled her into a hug. "We'll call tomorrow, and you can talk to her."

"Yay!" Annie tore across the hallway and out of sight.

"I wish I had their energy." She smiled at Daniel. "Would you mind hanging out with them for a few? Ev wants to talk to me."

The problems of the world, the problems with her family, and any other concerns that dared trouble her all faded away when Daniel's strong arms surrounded her. His earthy, masculine scent calmed frayed nerves, and the power of his chest provided shelter from the harsh realities of life. She could stay locked away in his embrace forever.

"I'll stay with the kids. Take as long as you need. If they start complaining about my story reading, though, I'll have to call in the expert."

She slid her hands up his back and around to circle his neck as she slowly kissed his cheek. The stubble on his jaw heightened the sensations and provided an exciting contrast to the softness of his mouth. Wanting to deepen the connection, she covered his lips with hers, eliciting a murmur of pleasure from him that resonated throughout their bodies. She loved the way his arms tightened and possessively held her body against his. They might not know exactly what "this" was, but she knew she didn't want it to end anytime soon.

"Thank you for everything tonight. You seem to have won over my big sis."

"Go talk to her. Be honest, even if it's hard. The truth hurts sometimes, but it's always better than lying to those we love."

Slowly, she extricated herself from his embrace. Time to face the music. She nodded toward her bedroom, where the kids were giggling as they engaged in a pillow fight. "Never let 'em see you sweat."

"Ouch!" He'd swatted her on the behind.

"Ditto." He winked as the normally present cocky grin plastered on his face.

Evelyn sat on the edge of the couch, a wineglass in her hand. "I opened a bottle. Hope you don't mind."

"Not as long as you share." She joined her on the couch, one cushion away, and poured herself a generous helping. No sense in prolonging the agony any longer. Might as well dive right in. "Am I still in hot water with Mother?"

Dull, blue eyes turned in her direction. "Do you really care?"

Daniel's words of advice rushed through her conscious thought. *Be honest, even if it's hard.* She chewed on her lower lip for a moment. "Not as much as I used to. Still, maybe more than I should."

"You always did have to do things your way. I think deep down there's a part of her that admires you."

The wine provided the only explanation for her sister's comment. "I think you're confusing me with you, big sis. You're the golden child."

"You really don't get her, do you?" She shook her head in disbelief.

Melodie took a long sip to buy some time to find the right words. "From my vantage point, she's never really gotten me. I've been one big disappointment after another to her."

"Mother is a bit of a control freak, if you haven't noticed."

This time the laughter wouldn't be suppressed. "Oh, I've noticed."

"She can't control you. No matter what she says or does, you still follow your own path." Evelyn graced her with a small grin. "You drive her crazy."

Finally! A small crack in Mother's suit of armor revealed. "We finally have something in common then. She keeps me on the edge of crazy. I've been jealous of you and your relationship with her my entire life. You both are so perfect. Hard to keep up."

Her sister's eyes darkened. "No one has it all together, Mel. I'm sure your boyfriend has filled you in on my imperfections."

She moved closer, not liking the sadness in her sister's voice. "He hasn't said a word. I asked for his help to slay my proverbial dragons. Though I'm curious, I have no idea what he said to you earlier tonight." She jabbed her sister a little with her elbow. "Mostly, I'm glad he came out unscathed."

Evelyn leaned back into the cushions, slim fingers holding the stem of her wineglass tightly. "He may be the only one tonight. I'm sorry, Mel. Sorry I wasn't a better big sister to you. Sorry I'm not as perfect as you've always believed."

A tug of compassion moved Melodie to close the remaining distance between them and pull her into an awkward hug. *I haven't been the best little sister either. Time to correct that mistake.* "Perfect or not, you're still my big sister, and all I've ever really wanted is to be awesome like you." She paused. "Okay, truth is, I'd love, just once, for Mom to have the same gleam of pride in her eyes when she looks at me. Then maybe I could put my jealousy to rest."

"Have you ever said that to her?"

"I..." Had she ever really said those words aloud to her mother? She'd thought it a thousand, maybe even a million times, but did they ever make it past her lips? "Maybe not."

"Then you should. Be honest with her, and remember why you drive her crazy. Her bark is worse than her bite."

Melodie raised one eyebrow. "I'd rather not test that theory, or maybe this is your secret plan to becoming an only child."

Evelyn chuckled. "You've figured out my evil plan."

Mel sipped some more of her wine, contemplating both Daniel's and Evelyn's advice. "You're right, though. I do need to stand up for myself and be honest with her. With Daniel around, I feel brave and want to share with her how I really feel—not during a screaming match—but in an adult conversation."

Evelyn sank farther into the couch, her eyes narrowing. "You really met him on a plane?"

The rich sound of her laughter filled the room. "I did, and to say we got off on the wrong foot is an understatement. I literally fell into him as I tried to let him into his seat."

"You must've found your footing because somewhere between Chicago and Dallas, you two fell in love or something."

"I don't know if this is love, but I like having him around. He's equally responsible for lifting me higher than I've ever gone and driving me completely insane, sometimes at the same time."

Evelyn's expression sobered. "Be careful, Mel. He has a little girl, and she is smitten with you. Don't get too attached if you're not sure this is something you want to go long-term." She turned her head toward the giggling coming from the back room. "May be too late already for not getting attached."

"Neither he nor I can say what this is, but we want to explore it." Melodie sat her glass on the table. She wanted to wrap this up while everything was going well, She needed to enjoy this small slice of happiness.

Her sister's gaze locked on her face. "He's in love, Mel. I've watched him with you and, most importantly, with Annie. No way does he bring her here to meet you and come to a family dinner without being head over heels in love."

Melodie stood. "I'm glad we got a chance to talk. I'm going to read the kids their bedtime story. Why don't you let Jason have a sleepover? I'll bring him home tomorrow."

Her sister sat back, crossed her legs, and sipped her wine. "If you promise you'll talk to mother soon, very soon."

Thoughts of having a heart-to-heart with mommy dearest set her pulse racing, but somewhere in the midst of the pounding, she knew the timing would never be better. Tom's unwavering support of her throughout her formative years, Daniel's powerful presence by her side, and Evelyn's softening toward her inspired confidence. "Yes, soon."

"Let me kiss my son good night, and I'll leave him in your capable hands." She pointed at Melodie. "No sugar for breakfast."

"No problem. We'll keep it simple and have donuts." Bantering with Evelyn was kind of fun.

Evelyn rolled her eyes. "No idea why I bother. You always do what you want anyway."

As her sister's statuesque figure moved down the hallway, Melodie hoped her newfound courage wouldn't turn out to be false bravado once face to face with her mother.

CHAPTER THIRTY-EIGHT

"And they lived happily ever after."

Daniel didn't even try to hide his smile as he considered the idea of a happily ever after with this woman. The warmth in his chest expanded, spreading heat throughout every limb. The vision of Melodie in grey gym shorts and a pink princess T-shirt surrounded on either side by sleeping angels inspired feelings never experienced before. Feelings he needed to handle before he slipped and did something totally crazy. *Like tell her I love her.*

"Can you make a pallet on the floor for Jason?" she whispered. "The extra blankets, pillows, and comforters are in the hall closet."

Moving closer to the bed, he lowered his voice. "I'm making one for Annie too. I'm not sleeping on the couch again tonight."

Her mouth opened to protest—this he could handle. Avoiding the sleeping children, he braced his hand on the pillow under her head and slid his lips over hers. The silence—golden, her mouth—amazing.

Moments later, she turned her head to break the kiss. "You're very adept at shutting me up."

Unable to resist, he slid the tip of his index finger over her lips, the touch returning her to silence. "Haven't heard you complain yet—one more quick kiss." *Damn, kisses are addicting.* "I'll get the blankets and be right back."

Less than five minutes later, his army training paid off, and he'd assembled two makeshift pallets on either side of the bed. He lifted Annie and kissed her forehead. "Good night, princess. Sleep well. The kingdom is safe."

He repeated the maneuver with Jason, leaving out the kiss. "You fought mightily, brave knight. Sleep well."

As cute as the kids were, their presence in the room only delayed his reward for slaying the dragons. He turned off the light and slid onto his side of the bed. His fingers ached to feel Melodie's skin. A few touches wouldn't hurt. Reaching under the covers, he caressed her bottom, the resulting murmur of pleasure music to his ears. Need and desire prompted him to push for a little more. Spooning her firmly against him, his hand slid higher and to her front. The fire in his belly ignited, demanding relief the moment his palm cupped her breast, teasing the tips.

Maybe they could move this party to the living room, bathroom...any room but here. "Mel?"

"Mmm, good night. Very tired...thank you for slaying my dragons." She moved closer into the "spoon" shape with him, breathed a sigh of contentment, and settled further into sleep. Any other time. Any other woman. Normally, this situation would've pissed him off. With Melodie, the physical ranked pretty damn high in importance. For the first time, though, something more demanded attention. He wanted peace or at least some version of happiness.

He snuggled in close enough for each breath to draw in the clean scent of her shampoo. Contentment rained down on him, and, in that very moment, he knew. Damn it all, and despite his best efforts, he'd gone and fallen in love.

Hours later, Daniel jolted awake, sweat clinging to his chest and limbs. Checking quickly, he saw that Melodie had turned on her side when he woke, but the gentle rise and fall of her chest showed she was still asleep. Drawing a slow breath in and then releasing it, he prayed the pounding of his heart wasn't as loud as it sounded in his ears. Otherwise, everyone would be awake in a matter of moments.

He rolled his shoulders in an effort to ease the tension. Each muscle in his body protested the movement. He hurt everywhere. The rock in his stomach weighted both his body and spirit. The vivid nightmares providing a painful reminder that, despite what Melodie said, he didn't deserve happiness. Looking at her sleeping form, blanketed in innocence and beauty, he also doubted he deserved her.

CHAPTER THIRTY-NINE

————

Saturday

"Auntie Mel! Wake up. Wake up. Wake! Up!" Jason bounced on the foot of the bed. "Did you marry Annie's dad?"

The bouncing and yelling she might've been able to ignore, but his question was another matter entirely. Forcing the sleep from her limbs, Melodie reluctantly pulled herself from Daniel's embrace. "Come here, sport."

Jason bounded into her arms and plied her with a good morning kiss. "Did you marry him?"

"What makes you ask such a question? You know I'd never have a wedding without you being there as the ring bearer, right?" She tousled his mop of brown hair.

"He was sleeping in your bed. Doesn't that mean you're married?"

She searched her brain for a way to explain her sharing the bed with Daniel without providing him anything potentially scarring or trouble-worthy when he repeated it. At seven, she had no doubts he'd repeat it.

Before she could answer, Daniel's gravelly morning voice joined the conversation. "You ever slept on your aunt's couch, buddy?"

Jason's eyes squinted. "Yes."

"Was it comfortable?"

The brown curls bounced as he shook his head. "No. Very lumpy."

"You and the princess here took up all the space on the floor, and my old back couldn't take another night on the couch."

Jason nodded. "Only place left was Auntie Mel's bed. Good thing it's big enough for both of you."

Melodie pulled Jason into her arms and started tickling him. "My couch is lumpy, you say? I'll show you lumpy."

The giggling woke up the remaining sleepyhead, and Annie joined the party. "Tickle me, Daddy. Tickle me."

Daniel smiled at his daughter, but it didn't reach his eyes. "Maybe later, princess. Daddy's tired this morning."

Melodie kissed Jason on top of the head. "Okay, you two, go get on the lumpy couch, and find some cartoons to watch. We'll be out in a minute to fix some breakfast. I'm pretty sure there are donuts in the cabinet calling your names."

Cartoons and sugar prompted the kids to leave the room in a hurry, leaving her alone with the man who'd played hero in the most erotic of dreams last night. The moment the kids cleared the door, she leaned over and kissed him on the cheek. "Did you not sleep well last night?"

His lips covered hers and made her forget for a moment what question she was asking him. His kisses ventured lower, the neckline of her T-shirt being pulled aside to give him access. Temptation engulfed her, pushing aside the adorable rug rats channel surfing down the hall. Physical and emotional need weaved together to form a chain of desire settling low and deep within her body.

"Daddy, we're hungry!" Annie's voice sliced through the building tension between them, and she regretted instantly his lips lifting from the swell of her breasts.

His eyes darkened. "I'm pretty damn hungry myself but not for donuts."

One more kiss. She needed one more kiss before she could tear herself away. Pulling his body flush with hers, the hard contours of his chest provided a comforting and welcome weight against her chest. "Tonight, Annie sleeps on the lumpy ol' couch, and you get the bedtime story you've been wanting."

Thoughts of the children dissipated the moment their lips touched. Pleasure mounted swiftly as his tongue swept across the seam of her mouth. With no hesitation, she opened to him, deepening their connection. Wanting more. Needing more.

"Auntie Mel! We're starrr-ving!" Jason's desperate proclamation forced them apart once again.

Her eyes closed as Daniel's fingertips slid over her highly sensitized and well-kissed lips. "Maybe Annie can stay with them tonight and give us an evening alone."

She laughed and sat up, fearful if she remained prone it would prove too difficult to resist pulling his body on top of hers for another attempt. "Just as well, I need to get ready and drop Jason off before work." Her hand covered his heart. "You will be here when I return, won't you?"

The strong beating under her palm increased, and his hand came to rest over hers. "I want to be with you as long as you want to be with me." She'd grown accustomed to him being here. She didn't want to think of how lonely this place would feel when he had to go home.

A quick kiss this time before she made her way to the kitchen. "Come and get it, kiddos. A breakfast filled with sugar and carbohydrates. Your parents will thank me later." She loved being the aunt.

Jason devoured the first few bites of his chocolate goodness while Annie remained ever the lady and nibbled at hers. Melodie could swear she witnessed a glint of amusement in the young girl's eyes as she watched Jason consume his breakfast. Once the first few bites were down, along with a few swigs of milk, Jason found his voice. "You should ask Mommy where she bought her couch."

Melodie sipped some of her coffee and tried not to think of Daniel using up all the hot water in the shower without her. "Why's that, sport?"

"Cause Daddy sleeps on the couch a lot of times. It must be more comfortable than yours."

Melodie thought to the number of times she'd seen her sister lately, rarely accompanied by her husband. Maybe Evelyn's life wasn't as accomplished and perfect as she let others, her family included, believe. "I'll be sure and ask her. Finish up your breakfast while I get ready, and then I'll take you home."

"Can't I stay? Puhlease?? I wanna play with Annie today."

Daniel stepped into the kitchen. "It's okay with me if his mom approves. We can take him home later after work. There's gotta be a park around here somewhere."

Sexy. Sensitive. Sweet. Smoking hot. His hair still damp from the shower and the flush of red on his tanned skin prompted her to not even care if he'd used up every single drop of hot water. A cold shower would be in order for her anyway. The desire to call in sick and spend the day with her pretend family overwhelmed her. It wouldn't do, though. Despite what her mother might think, she took her job and responsibilities very seriously. Add to that her promise to visit her mother and make another attempt to repair their relationship, today could rank pretty high on the total crap list. The thoughts cooled her ardor and provided focus on what needed to be done. "I'll call Ev and ask. Going to jump in the shower and get ready for work."

Before heading off to get ready, she squeezed Daniel's hand. When he looked up to smile at her, the dark circles under his eyes brought her concern for him back into focus. "You still haven't answered my question from earlier. Are you okay? You look exhausted." She winked at him and whispered, "I'm pretty sure I didn't keep you up all night."

He lifted their clasped hands and kissed the back of hers. "I'm fine. Go get ready for work. You don't want to be late."

And just like that—bam!—he'd shut her out. She'd gotten much better at reading him and recognized his behavior. Of course, it wasn't hard to remember as they'd been down this road before. She nodded and fought the urge to sigh. She didn't want to lose him again.

CHAPTER FOURTY

A lump the size of a donut hole rested firmly in her throat. The last four hours at work crept by with interminable slowness, allowing her to think of little else besides the conversation about to take place with her mother. Unwilling to put it off any longer, she pushed the button next to the door frame, sending chimes of her impending doom reverberating throughout the house and her heart. *I can do this. A conversation long overdue.* Confidence didn't fill her, but enough found its way into her limbs to give her courage to remain at the door.

"Mel, so good to see you."

The breath she'd been holding left her lungs. "Dad, how are you?" She pulled him into a hug. "How's Mom?"

They separated, and he smiled. "Not planning to divorce me, so I'd say the Alexander charm is still alive and well."

She couldn't decide if his words made her happy or sad. He'd told her before his vows meant something. For better or worse. From her perspective, he'd certainly been given a lot more of the worse than the better when it came to his relationship with her mother. "As long as you're happy."

He smiled and kissed her on the forehead. "Happiness isn't a feeling, baby girl. It's a state of mind, a conscious decision. Though, seeing you here, uninvited, makes me experience the feeling as well."

"Maybe Mom will extend her good mood and not try to divorce me either." She offered a small smile. What kind of grown woman dreaded seeing her mother? *This one, that's who.*

"She's in her office. Go say your peace. This has gone on long enough between you two. You deserve to find your happy state of mind."

He pulled her into a hug—a gesture she knew with absolute certainty she never wanted to outgrow. "I love you."

"Love you too." Her father's tender gaze held hers. "She loves you too. Never forget that, Mel. Even if she has a tough time showing it. You know how she is."

She exhaled slowly. She knew.

Her steps were slow. Every nerve ending, from the top of her head to the tip of her toes, coordinated their efforts to reduce her stride and delay the inevitable. The confidence building in her since Tom's death and meeting Daniel provided hope. She inhaled and exhaled deeply. She was ready.

Stepping into the formal and imposing study, she soaked in the power and affluence that radiated not only off the woman sitting behind the mahogany desk but off every piece of furniture and art. Marie Alexander, certified public accountant, business owner, formidable adversary, and timeless beauty. Finding and grabbing hold of her courage before it slipped down her pant leg and ran like a scared child screaming from the room, she located her voice. "Everything about this study suits you, Mother."

Marie looked up from her papers and removed her glasses. "It should. I hand selected and decided on every detail."

Melodie nodded. "May I come in?"

At her mother's gesture, she took her first step into the lion's den. "I confess. I'm surprised to see you. Social visits from you aren't really the norm."

Don't take the bait. Stay calm. Be honest, even if it hurts. "I want to talk—really talk. About you, me, and our relationship."

Marie's eyes narrowed. "I try to talk to you on a regular basis. You never seem interested in listening."

Because lecturing isn't having a conversation. "I have listened. The problem is, I can't get you to listen to me."

The older woman reclined, crossing her arms and legs. "Please, enlighten me."

Inhale. Exhale. "For starters, I am not now nor will I ever be a good cook. Not because I can't learn, simply because I don't want to. I enjoy research. It's how I learn. I do love having my head in a book and dreaming as it allows me to escape the harsh realities of life—a life, I might add, created primarily by a mother who reminded me often of never being quite good enough. I chose to be a librarian because giving children a love of reading opens up an entire world for them. When they can read, they can accomplish anything."

One more breath in and out. Almost done. "Finally, I'd like to provide some reassurance you did not fail."

Her last statement brought Marie to the edge of her seat. "I beg your pardon. What makes you harbor some crazy notion I think I failed?"

Melodie shrugged her shoulders, the worst over now. Anything from this moment forward would merely repeat a road they'd traveled many times. She'd grown used to her mother's unrelenting lectures and lack of understanding. "You wanted me to be like you, just as Evelyn is. Despite all of your cajoling, threatening, and humiliation of me from a very young age, you couldn't make me like you. Instead of accepting and loving me for who I am which, by the way, is a decent, hardworking woman, you focus on your failure to hand select and control every detail of my life."

Okay, now the worst was over, for real this time—she hoped. The air in the immaculate study held a heavy combination of relief and tension. Perhaps, for the first time in her life, she'd found the courage to tell her mother the truth. *And it doesn't even hurt that bad...yet.*

"What is it you want from me?" Marie slouched, a move Melodie had rarely, if ever, seen.

"Honestly?"

Marie rolled her eyes and offered the slightest quirk of her mouth. "I'm fairly certain you've been brutally honest with me thus far. Why stop now?"

"I want you to be happy, Mom. Happy with Dad. Happy with me. Happy with the family life gave you. I told Evelyn last night, during her impromptu visit, all I've ever wanted is for you to have the same look of pride in your eyes when you think about me as you do for her. Not because I'm like her or you, but because you're proud of me."

"Happiness is a choice, a state of mind."

She smiled as her mother's words echoed her father's. Maybe they had more in common then they let on. "Is your state of mind happy?"

Sitting forward, Marie folded her hands and leveled an intense glare in Melodie's direction. "Answer me this, young lady. Are you happy?"

Be honest, even if it's hard. She chewed on her bottom lip for a moment, waiting for a full measure of courage to pour over her tongue and allow her to speak. "I haven't been. I think maybe Tom's death taught me life is short, and there are no guarantees. In an odd way, his passing gave me courage to find the happiness I deserve."

"And you think this Daniel is your key to happiness?"

She may not be good at reading people, but she'd had a lifetime of dealing with her mother. This trap could be sighted a mile away. *Not this time, Mother.* She offered a smile and a small shake of her head. "No, as you and Dad say, happiness is a state of mind, not a feeling. The way Daniel makes me feel when I'm around him serves as a catalyst for me to believe I can have and, most importantly, deserve happiness. I've never experienced such conviction before."

"About damn time. I knew you had it in you."

Wait. What? Why? With no idea the direction her mother's thoughts would take them, she kept quiet and waited.

"You were right, at least in part. I have wanted you to be more like me, but not how you think."

No idea, not a friggin' clue. "Enlighten me."

"You've always wanted to do things your own way, but you failed to see that my pushing you was to help you be the best you could possibly be. Instead of listening to my instruction or giving me valid reasons why your way was better, you just buried yourself in your own little world and settled."

"See, this is what I'm talking about. You keep wanting me to be Evelyn. She's the attorney, the one who would argue a fine point to death. That's not my style. Besides, despite what you want to believe, I don't want to argue with you."

Before she could continue, Marie lifted her perfectly manicured hand to stop the argument before she even got started.

"Let me tell you a story, give you an example of what I mean. My parents wanted me to get married, have kids and stay home, and be a June Cleaver wife."

The thought of her mom being a June Cleaver housewife was not only impossible, but highly entertaining. "They must've loved when you went off to college with dreams to start your own business."

"They hated every second and made no secret about it either. They harassed me the whole summer after graduation until I left for college. Before I left, I set them straight on why I made the choices I did." Marie stood and moved to the front of the desk, only inches away. "Once I did, they understood why I had to do what I did. They still didn't like it, but I worked hard to better myself. It's hard for them to argue with success. You've never stood up for yourself. Conviction sets us apart. Your sister and I have it, and, God help me, I've been trying to instill it in you. I may not like your choices. Hell, I pretty much hate them. Today is the first time you've even tried to set the record straight." Marie's eyes widened slightly and one eyebrow rose into a perfect arc. "I'll repeat it again, to make sure you understand. My job is to make you better."

"You know what the problem with your logic is, Mother?" She'd hoped she could get her to understand, but a lifetime of always believing she was right and the success to back it up kept the indomitable Marie Alexander from seeing this one important truth.

"There isn't any, but I'm curious as to where you think the flaw is."

"Who gets to define what makes a person better? I know your definition works for you and Ev, but it doesn't work for me. I measure success, not from money or the number of plaques and certificates on my wall, but with the impact I can have on people's lives. My idea of better is instilling in children the belief that they can be whatever or whoever they want to be, regardless of what anyone else thinks. Our talk today has prompted me to be better in one area though."

Marie blinked rapidly for a few moments, but the firm set of her jaw and non-smiling arc of her mouth remained unchanged. "And what is that?"

"It is important to stand up for myself. I'm not going to argue with you about my choices, but if you really want to understand why I'm doing something, I promise to answer honestly if you ask me. As for everything else, maybe we can call a temporary truce and agree to disagree?" She really wanted to find at least a small measure of peace in the relationship with her mother. Better late than never.

Marie offered the smallest hint of a smile and a slight nod. "Temporary truce. Let's have a cup of tea, and you can tell me more about this young man serving as a catalyst to your happiness."

CHAPTER FOURTY-ONE

———

"I can't believe you've been bullshitting me all along." Daniel patted his very full stomach. A trip to the gym needed to occur sooner than later.

Melodie started clearing the table. "I'm not sure a casserole, salad, and dinner rolls qualifies as cooking. Occasionally, I like to prove to myself," she kissed him on the top of the head and winked at Annie, "and others I can still throw a meal together, if necessary."

Annie yawned. "Dinner made me sleepy."

Daniel picked up his daughter and held her close. "You had quite a day. Talking to Mommy and then playing most of the day with Jason."

The little girl smiled. "My brave knight."

"Let's get your bath, and then we'll make you a bed on the couch."

"But it's lumpy. You said so." Annie's protest reminded him of his lame excuse for sleeping with Mel last night.

"I'll put extra padding down for you, so you won't feel the lumps, okay?"

His heart expanded at the wary look in his daughter's eyes.

"Promise?" Bright blue eyes pierced into his, expecting nothing less than the truth.

"Promise."

"You run her bath, and I'll clean up in here." Melodie loaded the dishwasher.

"You sure? I don't mind helping out." Especially if finishing these chores got them into bed sooner.

"I don't mind."

He gave Mel a kiss on the cheek and started down the hall with Annie. Melodie had been quiet since returning from work and her parent's house. He'd offered to buy dinner for the three of them, but she insisted on cooking. Doubt started to form ranks around the walls of his heart. Tonight had felt so right, the three of them sitting down to dinner. He wasn't sure if she was quiet because of her conversation with her mother or if she was upset with him for not sharing this morning. His hand balled into a fist as the doubts started ticking through his mind again. Maybe he shouldn't have brought Annie. Had he been selfish and let his desire to see Melodie prompt him to skip several steps in the relationship and introduce her to his little girl? He'd wanted this so bad, but was he ready to bring her fully into his messed up world?

He turned the water off and gestured to the bubble-filled tub. "Here's your nightgown. You can play for a few minutes, then wash up, and let's get you ready for bed."

Annie's tired little eyes found his. "I like Mel. Can we stay here for a while?"

Yep, he'd gone and screwed the pooch, as his army buddies used to say. He pulled Annie into his arms. "I really like her too. We have to figure things out though. She has a job, and you have to go back to school. Mommy is looking forward to seeing you again soon. Daddy has to get started on his job too."

Big drops of water formed in her blue depths, rendering him completely incapable of promising her anything less than everything her heart desired.

"We'll figure it out, princess. Doesn't the fairy tale always promise a happily ever after?"

The watery eyes widened, joined by a radiant smile. "Yes."

"Then don't stop believing in a fairy tale ending, okay?" He kissed her forehead. "Now, get yourself cleaned up. I'm pretty sure you have some sand from the park stowing away and trying to turn you into the cutest sandbox ever."

"I know."

An hour later, Daniel pulled Melodie into his arms as they settled into bed. "Thanks for reading her a bedtime story."

"My pleasure. Kinda what I do."

"Do I finally get my bedtime story?" He needed her and the wonderful distraction she always provided from the negative thoughts swirling through his head. Not wanting to deny either of them for one more second, he slid his hand under the light blue silk nightie to palm the softness of her breast while his thumb circled the hardening tip.

She arched into his touch, heating his blood and sending each cell on a crash course for the same location.

As her fingertips grazed his chest, he growled, "Screw the story, I want the librarian."

Moving his body to cover hers, he paused for a moment to burn in his memory exactly how she felt under him. Damn perfect. There would be no controlling Mr. Hyde tonight. The gentleman and knight occupied too much time in the story lately. Time for a little fun. Lowering his head with the intention of fully capturing her mouth with his, she surprised him by capturing his cheeks with her hands and stopping his progress.

"Thank you."

His cocky grin emerged. "I'm just getting started, babe." To prove his point, he turned his head and placed a love bite on her wrist.

"Daniel."

The quiet tone of her words calmed his libido ever so slightly. "Sorry. I've missed you."

She pulled his face toward hers and rained the lightest of kisses over his face. Not exactly what he was looking for, but a decent start. The head on top of his shoulders told him to slow down, let her talk about what happened at her parent's house today, and then make the sweetest of love to her. The head below his belt disagreed and made a valid argument for why he'd earned a fun romp in the hay with his smoking hot librarian.

The heart in between those two opted for a compromise. "You're welcome. I know we need to have some quality conversation time, but…" Thrusting his hips against hers, he demonstrated how far down the path he'd already gone. He smiled. "I've been such a brave knight, slaying dragons and all."

His ploy worked, and her smile widened to the point her eyes crinkled. "Don't forget, and I quote, the most awesome babysitter ever."

Damn this woman and her irresistible charm. He collapsed on top of her and rolled them until her body rested completely on his. He laughed at her squeal of surprise. "Do not, and I repeat, do not bring up the children tonight. Jason's an awesome dude and way too smart for his own good. We'll talk about the kids, your parents, us...whatever you want to talk about after we take care of a little business."

He buried his face in the curve of her neck, alternating between licking, biting and sucking until her moans of pleasure ensured he had her full attention. The burning need to touch her, to feel every inch of her soft skin under his war-hardened palms heated to an unbearable level. Sweet Jesus, he needed her. The satin and lace joined his boxers on the floor.

Skin against skin. He'd wanted this for days now. Rolling them again, he looked down at the picture of perfection. With purposeful moves, he sought to taste and touch every inch of her body. His intent simple—consume her.

The gentle caress of her fingertips on his back and shoulders made him pause. He forced his eyes open to drown in green pools of emeralds, the very same jewels that bewitched him from the moment they'd met. He kissed her gently. "You okay?"

Her thumb slid across his bottom lip, curling the knot of desire even tighter in his gut. "Just being in the moment with you, savoring every second."

There was something more than lust or desire in her eyes, but dark lashes closed over the emeralds as her legs circled his hips, and he was gone...

CHAPTER FOURTY-TWO

———

Sunday

Melodie tapped her fingers restlessly on the marble counter, waiting for the coffee to brew. Both Daniel and Annie were still asleep, but rest proved a stranger to her most of the night. Last night would've been the most perfect night of her life, but concerns over Daniel's withdrawal, the dark circles and worry lines that creased his ruggedly handsome face kept her worried enough to prevent restful sleep. Oh, he'd been totally attentive while they made love but as they tried to sleep afterwards… She shuddered remembering the way his body jerked from what she assumed was a nightmare. The tormented look on his face as he endured whatever horrors played out behind his closed lids saddened her. She wanted to help him. Had offered to do so, if he would just let her.

Today.

Today she would press him to tell her the truth about the nightmares and promise him she'd see a specialist about her infertility. She would invite him to come with her and ask that she be allowed to come to counseling with him. They could be there for each other—find their own little slice of happiness in this world.

The hissing and gurgling from the coffeepot signaled the completion of the brewing cycle. "Thank God." A moment later the strong, hot beverage washed over her taste buds and heated the stone pit resting heavily in her stomach.

Unable to put it off any longer, as she didn't want Annie to be awake for this conversation, she poured him a cup and slowly made her way back to the bedroom.

The rock in her stomach did a flip-flop as she drank in the magnificent sight of Daniel. His body, a picture of perfection. The frown on his face and the deep furrow of his forehead indicated his mind was in turmoil. The ache in her heart intensified until the pressure in her chest stole her ability to breathe. The pure, agonizing realization washed over her. For the first time in her life, she'd allowed herself to fall in love. Her love for him demanded she try to help him get better. Though she thought it would be hard to argue against the merit of nightmare-free sleep, she wanted to avoid the same mistakes her mother had made by defining better for him. Pulling him down a road she'd never traversed would be wrong, but offering to walk with him would be better.

The smell of fresh coffee worked its magic, and a few minutes after entering the room, his long lashes fluttered open. His crystal blue eyes lit up as he came to awareness. "You brought me coffee in bed?"

She handed him the cup and smiled at the look of relief settling over his handsome face as he took the first few sips.

The lump in her stomach defied gravity and slid into her throat. She didn't want to mess this up. "I know I said it last night, but I don't think I had your full attention. Thank you for everything you've done for me and for my family. You have given so much of yourself, and we've shared so much of our pain. I've never felt a connection to another person like I have to you, almost from the moment I bumped into you on the plane."

He nodded but didn't smile. *Not good.* "I don't know how I can repay you for showing me how to live life and to face my dragons, even if you had to knock them down to size for me first."

Daniel set his cup on the table next to the bed and lifted her hand to kiss the back. "We've been good for each other."

She didn't like his use of the past tense. "Agreed, and I see not only a good future together but a great one." When he looked away from her, the lump in her stomach tripled in size. Placing her cup next to his, she reached out to touch his shoulder. The tension in the muscles clearly indicated he was anything but relaxed. "I know something is bothering you. I suspect your nightmares have returned. Talk to me. We'll figure this out together."

"There's nothing to talk about. This is something I have to work out on my own."

She blinked rapidly to stop the tears accumulating from slipping down her cheek. "No, you don't. I thought I was going to have to deal with my physical problems alone, but you offered to help me. I was thinking this morning as the coffee was brewing. We can set up an appointment for a specialist for me, and we can find someone to meet with, together, to help you through your challenges. I know they're not the same, but we both have things we need to deal with. Won't it be better to do it together?"

The nervous tension inside her body overwhelmed her small frame and escaped into the air from her admission. Waiting wasn't one of her strong suits either. Would her words get through?

Daniel's eyes hardened as he slid out of bed. "I appreciate the concern, Mel, really I do, but it's not necessary. I'm fine."

Following his lead, she moved to stand on the opposite side of the bed. "You told me the other day I needed to tell the truth, even if it hurt. Maybe you should follow your own advice. I may have a lot to learn when it comes to people, but I've developed a pretty good understanding of you. You're not sleeping, you've been withdrawn, and last night I watched you suffer through a nightmare. You are anything *but* fine, Daniel."

His body tensed, and the warmth drained from his eyes. "You have no right to judge me. You can't possibly understand what I'm going through."

She nodded. "You're right. I can't. But I want to understand—want to help you. Isn't that what people who love each other do?" Dear God, that's not how she wanted to profess her love for him.

* * *

Daniel's eyes widened. "You're trying to guilt me into therapy by telling me you love me?" That may be the lowest trick in the book anyone had every tried on him.

She shook her head as the tears began to fall. "I'm not trying to guilt you into anything. You want to define 'whatever this is'? Well, I can't answer for you, but for me *this* is love. That's right. I love you, Daniel. Because I love you, I want to share in life with you, both the good and the bad. You've given me a little of each along with a healthy dose of wonderful. Now I want to be there for you."

She loved him. Shit. He really didn't deserve that. She was everything he was not. Oh, he tried to be a good father, a good soldier, a good friend, but he'd failed. Annie had been growing up with an alcoholic mother while he was off fighting a war. He'd followed orders and demanded the same from the men who reported to him. His orders, his choices, had directly resulted in three men losing their lives. Last, but certainly not least, his green-eyed sexy wallflower had blossomed into the amazing woman standing in front of him telling him she loved him. He couldn't risk bringing her down with him. No. It was going to be hard enough holding himself together for Annie and making sure he didn't screw her up. He refused to take that chance. "You can't be there for me."

His heart began to break off into tiny pieces, cutting into his very soul at the sadness permeating the entire room. "I can. You just have to let me."

Whether she would ever believe him or not, he was doing this for her own good. "You can't because I'm leaving."

CHAPTER FOURTY-THREE

———

"You can't leave. Please, Daniel. Stay so we can work this out."

He closed the distance between them and kissed her on the forehead. "I'm sorry, Mel. I can't."

Her tears fell freely now. Damn. Damn. Damn. This really was for the best...wasn't it? "When are you leaving?"

"As soon as I can pack our stuff. I'll take Annie out to the car while she's still sleeping."

The thought of both of the women in his life reduced to tears delivered a crushing blow to his chest, making it difficult to breathe. He pressed his hands against the sides of his head, willing the pressure to ease. "When she wakes up, I'll try to explain everything to her."

"I need to say good-bye."

"No."

He forced himself to ignore the look of pain on her face.

"Please, Daniel. I know you're hurting, and I've probably gone about this all wrong. But, I really do care about you and Annie. I just want to say good-bye."

Stepping closer, his voice lowered. "If she sees you crying then she'll start crying. Not going to happen." His eyes found hers and locked them together for a moment. He needed to make sure she understood. "I hope you can forgive me for doing the right thing here. You're going to meet Mr. Perfect someday, rather than Mr. Messed Up, and you'll thank me for having the strength to leave you."

CHAPTER FORTY-FOUR

———

Melodie watched numbly as Daniel moved about the apartment collecting his and Annie's things. She wanted to say more but, really, what more was there to say? She'd told him she loved him and offered to walk next to him through difficult times. That was it—the most she had to give. And it wasn't enough. She wanted to scream at him, argue with him…hell, even throw something at him. Annie's peaceful, sleeping form kept her from doing any of those things.

Maybe the gift of argument was something to be treasured. Before she could come up with anything more to say, he'd carried Annie to the car and returned to grab their bags. Leaning forward, he kissed her on the forehead. "Good-bye, Mel."

She'd watched him pull away and stared after the empty space for several minutes before shutting the door and moving into her bedroom. Not wanting to be on the bed, she lowered herself to the floor in the corner of her bedroom, knees clutched close to her chest and head lowered. She let the tears fall until the supply had dried up, leaving a raw, empty ache deep inside her chest. Time passed by, either quickly or slowly, she couldn't be sure. Her cell phone buzzed a couple of times, but she was in no condition to talk to anyone right now. She'd call whoever it was back later.

Stacks of unread books hovered nearby on her nightstand, calling to her with their swan song. An invitation to lose herself in the pages and escape the pain reality served up on a regular basis. Why had she let herself succumb to Daniel's charms? Even worse, why had she agreed to let him stay here with his loveable daughter?

An incessant banging on the door proved much harder to ignore than a buzzing cell phone. She hugged her knees even tighter and tried to black out the images of Daniel carrying his sleeping angel out the door and out of her life.

"Mel, what the hell is wrong with you?" Her sister's voice entered the room only moments before she did.

Melodie sensed her crouch down next to her, the familiar smell of her perfume offered a small touch of comfort in the midst of the turmoil. "Where are Daniel and Annie?"

A fresh supply of tears from God knows where found their way to her eyes and spilled out onto her cheeks. "Gone."

"That sonofabitch left you again? I'll find him and rip him a new one." Evelyn morphed into full attorney attack mode.

"No, I made him leave, I guess." Her voice wavered, but the message made its way through.

Her sister's body nudged in next to hers as Ev made room for herself on the floor. The pleat in her immaculately pressed pants served as a vivid reminder of how completely opposite they were. Still in the grey shorts and pink T-shirt, a very damp pink T-shirt, her appearance was a stark contrast to her sister. Not that it mattered anymore...

"Tell me what happened." Evelyn put her arm around Melodie and pulled her closer in a half embrace.

"I messed up in a big way."

"How so?"

"I told him I loved him and wanted us to help each other through the challenges we were facing." The admission came with a quiet acknowledgement, the tear slipping slowly from the corners of her eyes. Honestly, how could there be any water left in her body at this point? Realizing she was now dampening her sister's silk blouse, she pulled back. "Sorry about the blouse."

Warmth infused her cold heart as a strong arm pulled her even closer. "It's a stupid blouse. You cry if you need to. I'll send you the dry cleaning bill."

The slight tease in her last statement prompted Melodie to lift her head enough to see her face. "Thanks for being here." *Having a big sister is nice.* "Why are you here?"

"I wanted to see how things went with Mother. I tried calling, but you didn't answer the phone or return my calls. A bad habit you have, I might add. I came after mass."

"Where are the boys?"

"With their father, something about a trip to Bass Pro Shop, I think."

At the mention of the store where she'd had dinner with Daniel, she buried her head back in the comfort of Evelyn's embrace. "I was going to call you later. As you can see, I'm in no condition to carry on a conversation."

Manicured fingers gently combed through her hair. "I'm going to give you about five more minutes to wallow in self-pity, and then we're going to get off this hard floor, have a cup of coffee, and figure this out."

Melodie wanted to argue but knew this time her sister was right. Not that she would admit that outright to her. Five more minutes didn't seem a reasonable time to process everything that happened between her and Daniel this morning. "Ten minutes?"

Evelyn smiled. "Seven and a half. Who says I can't compromise?"

Melodie closed her eyes but returned the smile with a small one. "You're a gem."

Exactly seven and a half minutes later, she was in the kitchen with her sister, watching as she made a fresh pot of coffee. "So, he left because he doesn't love you?"

"No, I'm pretty sure he left because he believes he doesn't deserve to be loved."

"Why?"

Melodie paused for a moment, not really sure this was her story to share. "Something happened when he was in Afghanistan working as a civilian contractor. He feels guilty for the role he played." She made eye contact with her sister, hoping to convey how serious this was without providing any more details. "Very guilty."

Several moments passed before her sister blinked and nodded. "OK, I understand that's his challenge. What's yours?"

This explained why her sister was a successful attorney. She never missed a detail. "I can't have children."

Evelyn's face registered surprise, but she quickly composed herself. "When did you find out?"

"The doctor told me about six months ago, right after Tom shipped out after his leave. The doctor and I have been trying different treatment options, but the scarring from the endometriosis is too severe."

Her sister pulled her into a strong embrace again. "I'm so sorry, Mel. The fact you can't have children isn't the end of the world. There are other options."

Melodie smiled sadly. "That's what Daniel said. I believed him...and you." She added. "I told him this morning I wanted to help him through his challenges just like he offered to help me through mine. I thought it was a perfect solution. He disagreed."

"And you listened to him?"

Evelyn's words struck a chord. She'd fought hard for him...for them. Hadn't she? "Not at first, but, unlike my family, I wasn't going to pressure him into trying to be or do something he wasn't ready for."

"Oh, save the dramatics. This isn't about pushing him to be better at something, this is about finding a way to show him love, and keep loving him until he believes he deserves it."

"I did try. I swear."

Evelyn hugged her. "I know, kiddo, but you can't give up so easily. Love is hard. Trust me."

Today, ironically, the childhood nickname made her feel loved rather than annoyed. "I'm not arguing, I promise. I just really am at a loss. He's refused my love and my help, taken Annie, and left."

Evelyn's eyebrow rose, "Are you doubting your big sister's ability to help you find a creative solution to this problem?"

Evelyn's words peaked her attention and brought a small smile to her face. "Your name on the door of a major law firm in downtown Chicago suggests there is no room for doubt."

Evelyn pulled herself to her full five-feet-eight inches and winked. "Then it's time to completely break out of your comfort zone, and do something different if you want different results." Her posture slouched a fraction. "Trust me—I know a thing or two about this."

Melodie remembered Jason mentioning his dad slept on the couch many nights. Maybe Ev's fairy tale life wasn't the happily ever after she portrayed. Soon, very soon, she'd ask her about the status of her marriage. First, she wanted her to continue this line of thought. "Well, you've picked the perfect time to suggest this as I've been slowly breaking out of that zone for weeks now."

"Good! Then here's what I suggest you do. Pull yourself together, book a plane ticket, knock on his front door, and park yourself in his living room until he admits he needs you and can't live without you." Evelyn smiled. "I'm pretty sure the law says if you stay long enough, you'll become his common-law wife."

"Let's say I want to do that. Other than the state, I have no idea where he lives." She wasn't even sure a cell number would help at this point. She could call, but this conversation needed to take place in person.

Evelyn chewed on her bottom lip, signifying deep thought. Mel grinned, remembering her picking up the habit at a very young age. Mother would always fuss reminding her of the "tell" being a show of weakness. Mel thought it made her appear more human and something less than a goddess.

Finally, Evelyn spoke. "I know a guy, an investigator. He owes me a favor. You make arrangements at work, and book your flight for Friday. I'll have an address for you by then."

Miracles never ceased. This particular miracle she had to thank Daniel for, as he served as the catalyst for the turnaround in the relationship with her sister. "Are you doing this because Daniel blackmailed you into being nice to me?"

Her big sister grinned. "A few points of order, little sis. First, Daniel isn't here, so there's no threat of blackmail looming over my head. Second, while I might not approve of his methods, he helped me see you in a different way—the way I should've viewed you all along. He stood up to me without flinching. There aren't too many people around with the guts to take me head on. I respect him."

"He's kinda great, isn't he?" *No, he's wonderful.* She was going to find him and make him see how amazing he truly was.

Daniel had handled her family flawlessly.

"Let's not get carried away. He's still a man, which means he possesses serious flaws. But, as far as his gender is concerned, he comes across as better than average."

Thinking of their last night together, Melodie's eyes closed. "Much, much better than average."

"On that note, I'm going to leave you to start the repairs on your red, puffy eyes. Judging by their current state, Friday may be cutting it close to be back to normal."

Melodie raised her hands in surrender. "I know. Tea bags and cold compresses followed by plenty of rest." And research on survivor guilt.

She felt the comforting embrace of her sister once more and a kiss on her forehead.

"You can do this, Mel. I believe in you"

What an emotional day. She'd finally experienced the pleasure of a closer relationship with her sister, and she'd lost Daniel. For the moment anyway... Her track record in the game of love currently stood at no wins and entirely too many losses. With a deep breath in and another out, hope and courage filled her heart. Time for a change.

CHAPTER FOURTY-FIVE

———

Friday

Melodie swallowed hard as she stood at the beginning of the small brick path leading to Daniel's front door. Five days—a lifetime—transpired since Daniel took Annie and left. No texts. No phone calls. No showing up at her door. This time she would be the one to take the initiative to set things straight. She liked that.

Evelyn, true to her word, called in a favor and provided his address. The modest house occupied a small plot of neatly manicured lawn. The one-story, grey home boasted a small porch with new wooden pillars holding the roof in place, a recent repair perhaps? Three concrete steps at the end of the small walkway would put her squarely in front of the white door leading to her fate. Well, she'd come this far.

A red Ford mustang—convertible, of course—adorned the driveway. The lump in her throat expanded as memories of staying out all night with Daniel flashed in her mind. In direct contrast to the muscle car, a pink bicycle with white and pink tassels decorating the handlebar leaned against the garage. She smiled. Daniel certainly operated as a man of contrasts. *Dr. Jekyll and Mr. Hyde.*

Time to see which of those two personalities would answer the door. Each step reminded her of drudging through a mud pit, laborious and slow. *No walking on sunshine today.* She opened the screen door, knocked, and waited.

Nothing.

She checked her watch, a little after two in the afternoon. He could be at work, but the car was in the driveway. She knocked again, a little more forcefully. Still nothing.

You can do this. Evelyn's words strengthened her resolve. She had nowhere to be until Monday morning. She'd wait. Longer than Monday, if necessary. This was it. He was her happily ever after.

Thirty minutes later a loud rumbling sounded at the end of the block. She stood, prepared to run, depending on the source of the noise. Then she saw him. Her bad-boy-turned-knight-in-shining-armor clad in jeans and a leather jacket straddling a cherry red, trimmed in black motorcycle. Talk about sex on wheels. Her body tingled in remembrance of his pressed against hers, sending her so high she had to look down to see heaven.

He pulled into the drive, removed his helmet, and slid off the bike with the grace of a panther. His fingers combed through the closely cropped hair—he'd cut it since he left. The sight of him eased the ache building in her heart from the moment he said good-bye. "Hey." Not eloquent but a start.

Her voice drew his attention away from the bike. "What kind of motorcycle is that?"

His face registered a mix of wariness and surprise. "Ducati. Best damn bike there is."

"I like it. Suits you perfectly."

He moved toward the front door, keys in hand. "I didn't expect to see you again."

She followed him onto the porch. "It seems Adventure Melodie decided to stick around. I've never been to Mississippi before. So I thought, what the hell. It's beautiful here, by the way. The colors are so vibrant. Pretty hot though."

He opened the door and stepped inside. His body blocked her ability to follow him in. Not wanting him to shut her out both physically and emotionally, she decided to appeal to the Southern gentleman. "So hot, in fact, that I've worked up quite a thirst sitting out here waiting for you to come home." She lowered her lashes and her voice. "Won't you at least invite me in for a glass of sweet tea or something?"

Daniel shook his head and grinned. "I half expected you to pull out a fan and try to mimic the accent with your routine. You really need to work on your Southern belle act."

A small crack in his resistance. Offering him a bright smile, she shrugged. "Hey I really am thirsty. Dehydration affects my acting skills."

The door opened the rest of the way, and he stepped aside. *One step closer.* "I'm out of sweet tea, but there's a fresh pitcher of lemonade in the fridge. Will that work?"

"Perfect, thank you."

A sweet shiver ran through her nerves the moment his fingers touched hers as he delivered the drink. A few sips of the tart liquid helped cool and calm her. "How's Annie?"

"She'll be home from school soon. She's adjusting well, mothering me quite a bit for an eight year old."

Thoughts of the blonde-haired, blue-eyed princess forced Melodie to wipe an errant tear from her cheek. "Sorry, I...I've missed her." She held his gaze with hers, willing him to see the love. "I've missed you."

He reclined on the cushions of the couch, a frown etched on his face. "She misses you too, along with the bedtime stories and Jason. She doesn't understand how milady can live without her knight." The blue eyes fixed a penetrating stare in her direction. "I don't know what to tell her."

Moment of truth. "I would tell her that while milady probably could, it wouldn't be what anyone would classify as living." Melodie reached out to touch his arm. "I don't want to go through the motions anymore. I want to be free to live life, and I want you to be as well. To prove it, I found you, flew all the way here, and waited thirty minutes in the hot, Mississippi sun for you. If that doesn't say I can't live without you, I don't know what does."

Her breath held as the entire world hung in the balance, well *her* entire world, as she waited for his response. He exhaled slowly and smiled. "All those books you read, and you quote something *I* said?"

The tension released its iron grip on her body, her breath escaping through laughter. "Well, you said something memorable that fit the occasion, so why not?"

He took her hand, holding it in between his. "I'm sorry I left the way I did. At the time, I really thought it was the best thing for you."

The air became trapped in her lungs again. "And now?"

He lifted her hand and kissed it gently. "And now, I've had time to let all the words you said to me along with a lot of lectures from Annie show me the error of my ways."

She could almost picture Annie's hands propped on her little hips explaining to her daddy why she knew and understood things he didn't. She was eight, after all. "What did she say?"

"The princess reminded me of how happy she—we—had been when we were with you. Every day she told me how much she loved me, and every day I've replayed you telling me you loved me. Every night, when I check on Annie, I keep thinking of those nights I found the two of you asleep on your bed. You both are so beautiful, and the angelic look on your faces as you slept helped me realize that while I might not be at a place where I believe I deserve you..."

"Daniel..."

"Hear me out, please. I might not believe I deserve you, but I know you both deserve the man you believe and want me to be. On my way home from work today, I stopped by my old shrink's office and made an appointment."

The tears wouldn't be held back any longer. As they streamed down her face, she pulled him into an embrace. She kissed his cheek and neck, before whispering in his ear. "I'm so happy for you. I know that wasn't easy. I love you so much."

He pulled out of her embrace, just enough so she could see his face. "I'm sorry that I didn't say this to you sooner. I love you, Melodie Alexander. Not just fairy tale love, but honest to goodness, real life, impossible to truly live without love. I've never met anyone like you, and, for the first time in my life, I've found true love."

She melted in his embrace the moment his mouth covered hers. The passionate heat from the kiss seared her very soul and branded her forever his. White-hot need sliced through her body as the tip of his tongue slid across her parted lips, deepening the connection. *So very good!*

Needing air, she reluctantly dragged her mouth from his. "God, I've missed you." To prove her point, she kissed him again between her words. "When I...thought I'd...never see you...again."

Finally, his hands cupped her cheek and held her motionless for a moment. "How did you find me?"

"Evelyn."

His eyes widened in surprise. "Big sister whose shadow you've lived in your whole life, Evelyn?"

She smiled. "No, big sister who my brave knight took head on and convinced her with his Southern charm and skill her little sister was a woman who deserved her respect. You earned her respect. Something I've tried my whole life to do and you managed it in one evening and on your first try."

The arrogant grin returned. "She thinks I'm hot shit, doesn't she?"

Melodie chuckled, "More like you rank better than average for your gender. That's the best compliment you'll get from her."

He moved closer. "Good thing I'm so into her little sister, or I might decide to prove to her I'm a helluva lot better than average."

"Oh, I already told her you were much, much better than average." She turned her head enough to kiss his slightly calloused palms. "Tell me I can stay, at least until we can figure this out."

Before he could say anything further, the door swung open. "Daddy, I'm home!"

CHAPTER FOURTY-SIX

———

Daniel tried to shift his focus from Melodie's question to his daughter. Holy shit, she really wants to stay. She's not just saying the words. She's backing it up with action. She deserved the perfect answer, but first he needed to tend to Annie. "Welcome home, princess. How was school?"

"School was...Miss Melodie?" The backpack dropped unceremoniously to the floor as her eyes shifted between the two adults.

"Mel came for a visit—"

"I came to say how sorry I was I didn't get to say good-bye and see if you would forgive me."

"I know." Annie proclaimed even though her face indicated confusion.

Melodie moved to kneel in front of Annie. "I've missed you and your daddy a lot. So much, in fact, I had to come see you both."

She nodded. "I know."

Daniel smiled. His eight-year-old daughter still knew everything, despite having so much more to learn. He admired her more and more every day. "Mel was talking to me right before you came home. She asked me if she could stay with us for a bit while we tried to figure out if we could maybe be a family someday. What do you think?"

Annie narrowed her eyes, focusing them on Melodie. "Will you read me bedtime stories and make Daddy laugh? He likes you. And I really want to play with Jason again."

Tears started their descent down Melodie's cheeks again. "Those are all very important things I want to do for you and your daddy."

Annie moved over to Melodie and pulled her into an embrace. "Don't cry, Mel. Daddy and I want you stay, and we can prove it."

Annie looked at him. "Did you show her, Daddy?"

Melodie wiped the tears from her eyes. "Show me what?"

He took her by the hand and led her into the bedroom. Without saying a word, he opened his closet and waited for her reaction. He wasn't disappointed. Those beautiful green eyes widened, and he swore the dullness covering them during their last encounter began to fade away.

Next, he pulled her over to the dresser and opened the top two drawers. Her hand squeezed his tighter. Finally, he led her to the bathroom and opened the medicine cabinet.

"Daniel, why? You cleared half your closet, half of the drawers in your dresser, and are only taking up half the space in the bathroom. Why?"

He scooped Annie up in one arm and used his grasp on Melodie's hand to guide them all to the king-size bed, depositing Annie beside him. "Annie and I had a lot of time to talk on the way home. She remained insistent she *knew* you were going to come visit us since, and I quote, a lady simply couldn't live without her knight. After a few days, she convinced me that in order to prove my love, I needed to make room for you in my— in our—lives."

Annie piped up. "I told him he needed to get rid of some of his stuff so we'd have room for yours."

Tears trickled down her face, even as those beautiful lips began to smile. Not exactly the reaction he'd wanted. "Don't cry, Mel. I'm not good with tears."

Melodie's smile formed completely. "I know." She leaned in and kissed him on the cheek. "This may be the sweetest thing anyone has ever done for me."

Momentarily forgetting Annie was sitting right next to him, he threaded his fingers through her soft waves and pulled her mouth to his in a crushing kiss. The hands of time turned back and filled his heart and body with pleasure as his tongue slid between her parted lips. She tasted lemonade tart, with the slightest hint of sweetness. Damn, she tasted good. The heat from her body infused him with warmth and fueled in him the desire to make her world as happy as she wanted to make his. He needed her. He loved her.

"Eeeww, gross!" Annie's exclamation broke them apart.

Daniel laughed as his forehead rested against Melodie's. "You know, princess, the couples in the fairy tales always kiss in the end."

Annie threw herself backward on the bed and put her hand over her forehead in dramatic fashion, "I know!"

Daniel kissed Melodie again, this time with less intensity. "Though it was Annie's idea, I agreed because I knew you believed me."

"Believed what?" She kissed him again as her hand slid to the back of his neck, holding him close.

Like I'm ever going to leave or let her leave again.

"Believed I wanted more—so much more than one night."

ABOUT THE AUTHOR

Nicole is a debut author with her contemporary romance series, *Heroes of the Night*. She has been an avid reader and lover of books from a very young age. Starting with Encyclopedia Brown, Nancy Drew, and Black Beauty, her love for mysteries grew and expanded to include romance and suspense. A Midwest girl, born and raised, her stories capture the love and laughter in her real world heroes and heroines.

To learn more about Nicole, visit her online at
www.nicoleleiren.com

Enjoyed this book? Check out these other romantic reads available in print now from Gemma Halliday Publishing:

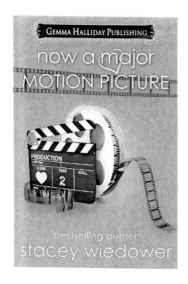

www.GemmaHallidayPublishing.com

CPSIA information can be obtained
at www.ICGtesting.com
Printed in the USA
LVOW12s0906110716

495771LV00001B/75/P